SALT
in the
WOUNDS

SALT
in the
WOUNDS

STORIES BY
MARK BLAGRAVE

Cormorant Books

 Canadä

The publisher gratefully acknowledges the support of the Canada Council for the
Arts and the Ontario Arts Council for its publishing program. We acknowledge the
financial support of the Government of Canada through the Canada Book Fund
(CBF) for our publishing activities, and the Government of Ontario through the
Ontario Media Development Corporation, an agency of the Ontario Ministry of
Culture, and the Ontario Book Publishing Tax Credit Program.

LIBRARY AND ARCHIVES CANADA CATALOGUING IN PUBLICATION

Blagrave, Mark, 1956 –, author
Salt in the wounds / stories by Mark Blagrave.

Issued in print and electronic formats.
ISBN 978-1-77086-385-9 (pbk.).— ISBN 978-1-77086-386-6 (epub). —
ISBN 978-1-77086-387-3 (mobi)

I. Title.

PS8603.L296S25 2014   C813'.6   C2013-908015-5
                                               C2013-908016-3

Cover photo and design: angeljohnguerra.com
Interior design: Tannice Goddard / Soul Oasis Networking
Printer: Trigraphik LBF

Printed and bound in Canada.

The interior of this book is printed on 30% post-consumer waste recycled paper.

CORMORANT BOOKS INC.
10 ST. MARY STREET, SUITE 615, TORONTO, ONTARIO, M4Y 1P9
www.cormorantbooks.com

For Sheila

Contents

Love You Like Salt

It started with a story at lunch. When I look back, I don't know why I was telling it.

"There once was a man who had three lovers and a heart condition."

"You're making this up."

"Yes. But it's a very old story."

"They all are."

"He couldn't decide which of the lovers to marry, for they were all wonderful women of excellent character."

"You can skip that part. Or come back to it with dessert. Where is that waiter anyway?"

"Is there something you want?"

"Nothing a waiter can give me."

It was exactly the kind of response that made me love eating lunch with Elizabeth. I couldn't fathom why some other man hadn't seen it too, why somebody so sharp had remained single. Her research, perhaps. She had joked more than once that she was married to Jane Austen.

"So anyway, he's trying to make his decision between these three women."

"Among."

"What?"

"His decision *among* these three women."

"Why among?" I was never ashamed to show Elizabeth that I was still willing to learn. It was, I liked to think, a difference between us.

"If he was trying to make his decision *between* them it would be quite a different tale. Sexier."

"I don't get it."

"Think about it. Where would he actually be, what would he be up to, if he was trying to make the decision *between* them all?"

"Oh. It's like 'lay' and 'lie.'"

"Sort of. In spirit. Not grammatically. Anyway, it's not that kind of story, Martin."

"You don't even *know* the story yet."

"You said it's very old. Okay, so how does he decide? *Among* them?"

"He says for each of them to bring him a gift."

"That figures." She reached for the salt and sprinkled her seafood crepe for the third time. "With you anthropologist-types it's nearly always about gifts somewhere along the line."

"Each of them is to bring him the one thing that she thinks is essential to life. And then she's supposed to explain how her love for him is like that thing — you know, essential for life."

"Right. I see. Is this guy a king, maybe? Some old guy called Lear?"

"No. Could be. Anyway, so the first woman …"

"Does she have a name?"

"Probably. But not in the story."

"They never do."

I braced myself for a rant on the effacement of female identity, but Elizabeth said nothing more. She seemed a little tired. I made a note to myself to ask her about it after my story was finished. "The first woman brings him Viagra."

"Jesus. He isn't using nitro for the heart condition is he? They can be fatal together, you know."

"I don't know. Not in the story. So you can't take Viagra with nitro? Who knew? The Viagra is only a symbol anyway. I thought you English-lit-types knew all about those."

"They go in and out of fashion. What's it supposed to stand for?"

"It stands for increased circulation, she says. She tells him that healthy blood flow is crucial for life — for his heart, see; and that her loving will keep him always fit, with his blood circulating nicely. What's the matter, Liz? You're very pale."

"I'm okay." But she pushed her plate away with a whole scallop still peeking out from a roll of crepe.

"So he thanks her and they kiss a bit and he goes ahead and tries out her present and …"

"I get it. So what does the second woman bring?"

"The second woman brings him an Armani suit."

"Folk tales have sure changed."

"And she says the suit will keep him warm, just like her love will keep him warm. Oh, and respected too."

"Her love?"

"The suit. Both, maybe. Anyway, he tries them both on. You know. If you're not going to eat that scallop ..."

"What scallop?"

"On your plate."

"Is that my plate? I guess it is. Help yourself." She shovelled butter onto the roll she had said she couldn't eat with the soup. Her hand twitched. The roll bounced on the floor. "Shit."

Her upper lip was beaded with sweat.

"Liz?"

"And what about number three? What does she bring?"

I knew this game. The nothing-is-happening-here game. I had played it often enough with my parents in their later years. Every time I visited. "She brings him a plain old pine board with a pile of salt on it."

"Salt."

"So of course he's furious. 'What have you brought me?' he says, 'Something worthless and unnecessary! And dangerous. I have a fuckin' heart condition. Salt could kill me.' And he sends her away."

"How does he manage to choose between number one and number two — the Viagra and the Armani? Which one does he marry?"

"Forget it. That's not where this story goes. This story follows the one who he sends away."

"They always do."

"She goes with great sadness."

"And wailing, and grief among the people?"

"Probably. Yeah. She walks and she walks and she ..."

"I think that *I* have to go, actually, Martin."

"What?"

"To go now. Right now."

She had gotten to her feet, but then sat back down hard. I was only just able to catch her head before it hit the table. Her brow was clammy and cold as ice.

IT WAS NEARLY TWO months before I was able to get Liz to agree to another lunch. The term was almost over. To each of my clockwork Monday calls inviting her, she pleaded other commitments, deadlines for some of the Jane Austen work. But I soon learned it was more than that. I happened to bump into a mutual friend who is on the medical faculty, and he filled me in.

"It's Addison's."

"What's Addison's?"

"Disease. That Elizabeth has."

"Joseph Addison? *The Spectator* Addison?" I don't know why I thought this might actually be reassuring for Liz.

"No. A doctor. Nineteenth century."

"Is it serious?"

"It's a condition of the adrenal glands, the adrenal cortex really. Things stop doing their jobs."

"So she's low on adrenalin. Who isn't these days? We could all use more energy."

"Something called aldosterone is the big problem."

"I've never heard of it."

"Doesn't make it any less important. It tells the kidneys how to regulate sodium levels."

"Sodium, as in salt?"

"Her kidneys are basically wasting sodium. They can't stop her from just pissing it away. Literally. They can't stop because there's no aldosterone to tell them to. It results in hyponatremia. Like what happened to Napoleon's army. The brain doesn't like it."

"Spilling salt. Like Judas."

"What?"

"At the Last Supper. Never mind. Will she be okay?"

"The usual treatment is prednisone. And she'll probably be told to carry a syringe of hydrocortisone for emergencies. How have you been, anyway?"

I wouldn't have told this guy, even if there were anything to tell. If I did, the whole faculty would know all about it in two days.

When Liz was still at the please-wait-to-be-seated sign, looking around for me, I thought she must be playing at being in a B movie, standing in some lighting effect created by the Venetian blinds or the hanging plants in the windows. But as she sat down I realized that the dappling was actually on her skin itself. She caught me looking.

"It's part of this thing I have. My pigment's all fucked up. I'm thinking of moving out of Jane Austen into something more trendy. Post-colonial, maybe. New qualifications.

I'm black and white, and could be read all over." When I failed to laugh, she said simply: "I don't want to talk about it. It's boring. Let's order."

We chose exactly what we did the last time, without discussing it before or commenting after. Once the waiter had shuffled away, she reached across and put her hand on my forearm. I liked the touch. We almost never touched. I was about to say something about it when she asked, "Where were we? She was walking."

"Who?"

"The rejected lover. The one who was sent away. Your story."

"Liz."

"She walks and she walks …"

"Fine. She walks and she walks …"

"Barefoot? It's usually barefoot isn't it?"

"… until she comes to an inn. And there she meets this fabulous chef."

"Better than the guy here? I thought the vegetables were limp last time. Then again, so was I."

"The best chef in the world. And he offers to teach her to cook."

"What did she do before?"

"We don't know. It doesn't matter. She learns to cook and she becomes the greatest chef in all the whole wide world."

"What about the guy who taught her?"

"He's happy to see his student surpass him."

"I doubt that."

"She becomes so famous she's invited to cook for important people all over the place. She's in huge demand."

"Oh. Of course. I see where this is headed. She's invited to cook for the lover who rejected her, right?"

"You *have* heard this."

"No. Tell me. I like the way you tell them."

"Yeah. He's having a big feast because he's getting married. To one of the other two. You're right, you know, it is a bit of a problem that we don't know which one he chooses. Anyway, he's marrying one of them, and the one who he rejected at the very beginning, she cooks up all these beautiful dishes."

Our soup arrived. Liz watched me watching her salt it, but I refused to look away. Maybe I could force her to talk about it. Her hand twitched and the salt shaker rolled across the table.

"Good thing I'm not superstitious," she said. "What, Martin? I dropped the salt. Aren't you ever clumsy?"

"Can we talk about it?"

"You mean like how I will lose out on one day in Paradise for every grain that got spilled?"

"You know I don't."

"I'm sick. I have this thing. It's boring. You like to read, Martin. I'll write down some websites. Let's eat lunch. Our soup's getting cold. So the jerk is getting married and he throws a big party, and the woman he sent away cooks up all these terrific things."

"And they're brought out from the kitchen. The tables are groaning with them."

"Wouldn't you love to see a groaning table? Just once. Like something out of Dickens. The rich people in Dickens."

"Or what Mrs. Bennett plans for Bingley." My attempt to flatter her with an Austen reference appeared to have no impact at all. I wondered why I had bothered to re-read the damn book. After a minute, I went on. "Everybody's thrilled. Finally, the king's very favourite dish arrives."

"So he *is* a king?"

"Didn't I say so? So his favourite dish arrives, and, grabbing up a spoon, he tastes it."

"It's good?"

"He goes nuts."

"It's that good?"

"He goes apeshit. I mean, he really loses it. He is absolutely furious."

"You mean it's *bad*? Did she poison him? Serves the bastard right."

"'This dish has not been *salted*!' he screams."

"You're kidding. But shouldn't he be on low sodium anyway? His heart condition and everything ..."

"'This has not been salted! Bring the cook before me!'"

"What, so he can have her beheaded?"

"Sure. I guess. He's mad enough. But anyway she just strolls into the hall not a bit scared."

"I think I like her. Gutsy."

"'Why did you forget to salt my favourite dish, you

careless bitch?' says the king." I stopped then. "Actually, it's a pretty stupid story. Let me start a different one."

"Let's finish this one. I think I know how it plays out. The king yells at her. And the girl replies, 'You drove away your most caring lover because she thought that salt was such a valuable thing. Maybe now you can see she was not so wrong!' And with that the king recognizes her as his long-lost daughter, and they embrace, and the wedding is doubly joyful."

"Just a minute. His daughter?"

"Isn't that right?"

"I said lover."

"Did you? Anyway, the point is that the guy learns how important salt is. That's what matters, isn't it? That everybody needs salt. Nobody should take it for granted. Does she ever explain to him how it is that her love for him is like salt and all that?"

"She doesn't have to."

"Right. Everybody knows that."

We ordered dessert and then coffee, talking about what was going on with our work but never returning to the subject of Liz's health.

Neither of us had a class in the afternoon and we found ourselves wandering along the waterfront. It was one of those March days when the sun promises more than it can deliver, and Liz began to shiver. I wrapped my arm around her shoulders. Before I knew it we were kissing. The biggest surprise was how natural it felt.

THEY BECAME A WEEKLY thing, our lunches and the lazy afternoons that followed in Liz's apartment or in mine. We were careful to agree each time that it was nothing serious. Friends with privileges. Sometimes I worried about the effect our lovemaking might have on her condition, but I always thought better of it just before I asked. In fact, she seemed to get better as the weeks went on. Her appetite came back, her skin warmed up, she had more energy and fewer headaches. Finally, I even decided to credit our weekly trysts for these improvements. And I wondered even more why some other man had not already snapped Liz up.

As the term ended and the rhythms of the teaching year gave way to those of summer and research, we went cold turkey. Our afternoons together dropped overnight from regular to non-existent. She spent a couple of months in Britain, working on some new idea about how Austen's writing was affected by her ill health. I travelled to Sardinia for a few weeks, to walk in the footsteps of Robert Graves. The rest of my summer was devoted to supervising three students I had hired on various grants. I had to remind myself daily that the luck I had had in actually landing all three grants I applied for was not something I could decently complain about to my colleagues. Fortunately, my work with one of the assistants, a young woman named Anneke, blossomed into one of those late summer romances that give people new leases on life — when they don't get them fired.

It was Elizabeth who made the first call in September.

Reluctant as I was to give up a lunchtime with Anneke, I agreed to meet the Tuesday after Thanksgiving. The usual place.

"So, once upon a time ..." She began as soon as we were seated.

"Just a minute. You're telling the stories now?"

"I didn't know I wasn't allowed."

"Of course you're allowed. It's just —"

"We literary types are interested in stories too, you know. Anthropology doesn't exactly *own* storytelling."

"It's just a change, that's all. New territory."

"Not for me."

"For *us*. Go ahead. Start again."

"Once upon a time there were two brothers. One was rich and an asshole and the other was poor and kind. Have you heard this one before?"

"How can I tell from that? Half the stories in the world start that way. More than half."

"One day — it was just before Thanksgiving — the poor brother and his wife discovered they had nothing to eat."

"Speaking of which, didn't they use to give rolls with your soup here?"

"Now you might well ask how do they just suddenly discover that they have nothing to eat? They're poor. They've always been poor. They must have seen it coming. Anyway, one day they discover they have nothing to eat, and, because this day happens to be just before Thanksgiving, that bothers them more than it might some other day."

"Sure, it's like feeling pressure to be giddy at Christmastime."

"Okay. So the wife says to the poor brother, 'Why don't you go ask your rich brother for some help?' Well, the guy is reluctant because his brother is always so mean to him. Did I mention that the brother is an asshole?"

"I think so. Maybe the poor brother is lazy and doesn't deserve to be rich."

"He's not a bit lazy. And nobody deserves to be as poor as he is. Maybe he's a little reticent, reserved, but he's not lazy. Anyway his wife reminds him that his rich brother killed a turkey just the other day, ready for the holiday, and she persuades him to go ask for some meat. Well, fowl, I guess."

"Folk tales don't usually bother with those kinds of distinctions. It's all meat to them. Do you think they've always put pollock in these crepes? I don't remember the menu being so specific about the ingredients before."

"How did the grants work out this summer?"

"The grants? What about your story?"

"It obviously doesn't interest you. Maybe later."

"The projects all went fine."

"I heard that one of them went quite a lot better than fine."

I couldn't believe I was actually blushing. But then I shouldn't have been surprised to find I felt more ashamed about it with Liz than with any of the half-dozen other colleagues who by then knew about Anneke. It was just that I had convinced myself to feel no guilt. What Liz and I had done in the spring was an interlude; that was all. We were both very clear. "And the Austen?" I asked.

"I'm not sure it led anywhere. Made me feel better though."

"Better?"

"You know, what with my Addison's and her Addison's, seeing that it probably had no effect whatsoever on her writing. That was my conclusion."

"Jane Austen had Addison's?"

"Maybe. Probably. There's pretty good evidence."

"Last spring, you never said."

"I thought it was common knowledge."

"You didn't want to talk about it."

"That too. I'm still waiting to hear about your projects."

"Let's get back to your story. So does the rich brother give his poor brother some turkey?"

"You know he does. A giblet. He doesn't like giblets."

"Nobody does. What are giblets anyway? Which organ?"

"It doesn't matter. He gives him a giblet and tells him to go see the local wood goblin."

"A 'wood goblin'? So this is not around here, this story. Why doesn't he just take the meat home to his wife?"

"Because he's an honest upright law-abiding … well, you know the type. He does what he's told. He sets off to find the wood goblin, and along the way he meets three guys with chainsaws."

"I saw this movie."

"I would have called them woodcutters only you were such a prick about the goblin."

"And what do the guys with chainsaws tell him?"

"That if he gives the wood goblin a gift then the wood goblin will have to give him a gift in return. That's the way this wood goblin rolls, apparently."

"They're mainly like that."

"The woodcutters tell the poor man that the wood goblin will offer him silver and gold but he shouldn't take any of that."

"But that way he could buy a turkey. And a pumpkin pie."

"They tell him to hold out for the goblin's millstone."

"His wife? No, that would be his ball and chain."

"Ha fucking ha. His actual millstone. Like for grinding stuff. When he gets to the wood goblin's place … Okay. I'm going to give the wood goblin a name because I can't stand to hear myself saying wood goblin this many times. He's Bob."

"Thank god he's not a hobgoblin."

"Bob smells the giblet a mile off and by the time the poor man gets to his hut Bob's beside himself with hunger. 'I haven't had any meat for thirty years,' he moans. 'Let me have a bite.' The poor man tells him that it's only giblet, but he says he doesn't care just hand it over. So he does and the wood gob — ah, Bob gobbles it down."

"Then he offers to give the poor man a gift."

"Right, just like the guys said he would. Silver, and the poor man says no. Gold, and he says no again even though it nearly kills him. Precious stones. His Betamax."

"You see, now that kind of embroidery just ruins it."

"You can have Viagra and Armani in your story and I can't have a VCR for mine?"

"Not an obsolete useless one."

"Finally Bob says, 'Look, I've made you some pretty sweet offers here. What's the problem?' And the poor man says 'I want your millstone.' And Bob says 'We're not talking about my heavy responsibilities and cares here are we?' 'Your actual millstone,' says the poor man."

"Nice touch."

"Thanks. Bob is an honourable guy, for a wood goblin, and he did eat the giblet, so he knows he has to give the poor man a gift. 'Okay,' he says, finally, 'Take the millstone. Do you need the manual?' But he can't find the manual, or the warranty either, so he just gives the poor man a quick summary of the instructions. 'This is a magic millstone and will grind out whatever you wish for. Just make your wish and then command it like this: Grind, my millstone. It will keep grinding out what you wish until you command it to stop. For that, you say these words: Enough and Have Done. Got it?' The poor man nods and heads off home with the millstone. And no, it isn't around his neck."

My cellphone rang. *Eine kleine nachtmusik.* Very obnoxious, I am told.

"I have to take this."

"It's Mozart calling?"

"Um, Anneke." And I blushed to my roots.

Elizabeth said she had to use the bathroom anyway and excused herself. I was still on the phone when she returned. I suppose that to an outsider the conversation would have sounded teenaged. Liz gave me a quick peck on the cheek and fled. She had almost finished her crepe.

I CALLED HER THE same night. Told her I was sorry about getting the phone call, but I also wanted to know why she left so suddenly. She offered to send me money for her half of the bill. I hung up. It was a ridiculous quarrel, I thought afterwards. Like old married people.

Anneke went out of town with her friend Sherry a few Tuesdays later and I decided to invite Elizabeth for lunch. Not at the restaurant this time — the memory of whatever it was that happened there was too fresh. We would get fish and chips at a stall in the City Market and eat them in the glassed-in atrium. That way, we would each pay for our meal before we got it, and if she left before I did it would hardly seem strange at all. And I wouldn't be out twelve-fifty.

She was late. I got tired of waiting by the fruit stand, so I wandered along to the gourmet foods place. When she tapped me on the shoulder I was reading the back of a cylinder of fleur de sel: "*Tout l'art du saunier est d'être patient pour recueillir avec dextérité, le moment venu, ce cadeau fugitive de la nature.*"

"I thought you were going to be by the fruit."

I put the salt back on the shelf as though it was hot. Or porn.

The atrium was busy, but there was one table in the corner. It had not been wiped. We flicked the crumbs off with a paper napkin and Liz blew a hill of salt onto the concrete floor.

"You look well. Younger, I think. How can that be?"

I didn't know what to respond. I was shocked at how unwell she looked. "You were telling me a story."

"Like Scheherazade. What was I buying time for?"

"The poor man had the magic mill. He took it home?"

"Of course. His wife was beside herself. She had given him up for dead."

"He'd only been gone a few hours."

"It's how all those folk-tale wives are. They worry very easily. You should know that, professionally."

"You're right."

"So the poor man tells her where he's been and what he's done, and then he puts the millstone on the table and commands it: 'Grind, my millstone.' And it starts producing this fabulous feast."

"Better than the cook made for her lover in my story?"

"Different. Magic. Not so human. Anyway, the poor people aren't picky, so they eat and eat until their stomachs are about to burst. 'Enough, and have done!' the man commands, and the millstone stops grinding."

"He could get it to grind out some antacid."

"He likes being full. He likes having heartburn. It's a luxury. After they have had enough to eat for a few days, he gets the stone to grind out some new clothes for them, and then a living-room set and an entertainment centre, and then a house to put it all in."

"What do the neighbours think?"

"We don't know. But we know that the rich brother is pretty mystified. He can't figure out how his brother got to be so well off all of a sudden. So he pays him a visit."

"And the poor brother — sorry, the formerly poor brother — tells him everything, right?"

"Would you?"

"No. But he does, doesn't he? Because he's so noble and good and everything."

"You make it sound like you mean he's stupid. Yes, he does tell him. Why shouldn't he? He tells him about his visit to the wood goblin's and how Bob ate the giblet and then offered him a gift in return. He tells his brother how he would have been proud to see his negotiating skills in getting the millstone. The rich brother pretends not to believe that a magic millstone could grind out all the fine things he sees around him at his brother's new house, so the millstone is brought out. And the poor brother commands it: 'Grind, my millstone.'"

"And it churns out a feast for them?"

"Sure, if you like. So of course, when he sees what the millstone can do, the rich brother wants to buy it."

"But it's not for sale, is it?"

"It was a gift. And besides, although he has enough right now, the poor brother remembers the old days and he wants to hang on to the means of production."

"I've been waiting for the Marxist touch."

"The rich brother begs him to lend him the millstone."

"Just a minute. I should have thought of this earlier. There's only one millstone?"

"That's right."

"How does one millstone grind anything? Don't you need two?"

"It's magic."

"Doesn't it get lonely? Without another one to rub up against?"

"The rich brother reminds the poor one that it was the gift of the giblet that made Bob hand over the mill-stone, and that it was he who provided the giblet in the first place. So finally the poor brother decides to loan it for one day."

"What can it hurt?"

"I'll take that as rhetorical. The rich man grabs the millstone and runs for his boat."

"Forget that this millstone seems mighty light — why does he take it to his boat?"

"You'll see. He loads it on his boat and sets out to sea."

"To sea? Wait a minute. Is this the fish and chips talking?"

Liz looked at her watch. We both knew that she didn't have a class to get to. She never teaches in the afternoon. "It's been lovely, Martin. I have to run."

"What about the end of the story?" But she had already started to move off. As I dumped the garbage from our trays into the bin, I saw her disappear beyond the cheese stall.

I KNEW THE END of the story, of course, but for some reason I needed to hear Liz tell it. I left half a dozen messages on her machine. I did not try email. In one of those weak moments that aging lovers have, I had given Anneke access to my account. This business between me and Liz had nothing to do with her, would only confuse her.

One day I bumped into the doctor-friend, hoping and fearing at once to hear that Liz's condition had worsened. But the man knew nothing, and seemed surprised to be asked. "I thought you two were ..." he said.

Finally, I went to her apartment. It was after midnight. That way, I knew she would not be out at the library or her office.

Liz showed no surprise at seeing me. She answered the door wearing a man's white dress shirt and a pair of slippers. I had trouble tearing my eyes off the dappled legs long enough to recognize the shirt as one of mine. I remembered then how she had talked me into going home in my T-shirt one day in the spring, leaving the dress shirt to be mended. I noticed she had not mended it.

"Would you like coffee?"

"A drink maybe. If you have any."

"Wine okay?" She opened a bottle of Shiraz, poured it into tumblers. "Stemmed glasses can be a problem when my hands shake. These hold the same amount. I checked once. What shall we drink to?"

She was sitting in the armchair opposite mine, with one leg tucked up underneath her. All I could think about was whether she was wearing underpants. The smell of her, the taste of her. "Your story."

"You want to drink to it or hear it?"

"One and then the other."

"In which order?"

"Doesn't matter." I wished desperately for a sudden gust of wind in the still room, something that would lift a shirttail, tell me what I wanted to know.

"The rich man had the magic millstone, right? And he was headed out to sea? Is that where I'd gotten to?"

"And then you left. Why did you leave?"

"So he rows out to where there is a bunch of fishermen hauling in their catch. Is the wine okay?"

"Perfect."

"He looks at the fishermen and he thinks that if a man could manage to supply them with salt right then and there he would be a rich man."

"This is before refrigeration then? They salt the fish right on the boats? Isn't he already a rich man?"

"You're the one who wanted to hear the end. You can never be too rich."

Or too thin, I thought, looking at the line of Liz's neck as it disappeared into my shirt collar. "Go ahead."

"So he says to the millstone: 'Grind, my millstone. Make me as much salt as you can.'"

"And the millstone starts grinding out salt."

"Mountains of it. The purest whitest salt you could ever imagine. It keeps coming and coming. Pretty soon, the rich man realizes it's making so much it's going to sink his boat."

"So he begs it to stop."

"But he hasn't been told the words. He doesn't know the magic command. He tries the obvious ones like stop and desist and cancel and undo. You don't mind that I'm wearing your shirt, do you?"

"Is that my shirt?"

"It's just that you left it here, and then by September I didn't know how to give it back. You know."

"I do. Look, Liz, I'm sorry if I misunderstood what we —"

"We were always very clear. It wasn't anything but a diversion. Friends with privileges, that's what we said. I need another glass of wine. Can I top you up?" As she crossed the room for the wine bottle, I squinted to see if I could detect a trace of fabric beneath the shirt, but the light was not right and I remained none the wiser.

"Then he tries in different languages to make it stop, and then he tries everything he's ever heard in a fairy tale, every incantation he can think of."

"But nothing works."

"Once he has started it grinding he can't find the words to make it stop. So the boat sinks, and the man drowns."

"And the millstone keeps on grinding."

"Turning out salt at the bottom of the ocean. To this day. And that is how the sea got salty. And now, if you don't mind, I think I have to go to bed." She had downed her second glass of Shiraz in two gulps, and was already turning out lights. When the room was dark, she said simply: "Are you coming?" and then she disappeared.

I stood there in the blackness, trying to remember the magic command to make the millstone stop.

Transit of Venus

Petra

"JUST SAY YOU'LL TRY it," I say.

"But I don't see —"

"It's not as if anything else has been working." I put down my fork for emphasis. I am also happy to have the excuse. We have been eating a steady diet of fish, rice, and coconut for a week. I suppose there are parts of the world where this would be the accepted routine, but I'm dying for a hamburger. Or a sausage. Neither, however, is recommended in what I've been reading about fertility foods. If I expect Bill to stick to the rules, then I guess I must too.

Bill has also put down his fork. He takes a long drink from his wineglass. "Half my life I've been lectured at to avoid salt like it's poison. You yourself have even nagged me about cutting down, and now you're saying we should be gobbling it up. What would the doctors —?"

"Doctors don't know shit. Medical science is just

another form of superstition." Of course I don't mean it, and I never talk like this, but I am becoming what's called a desperate woman. Running out of options. It is not, though, the right thing to say to him, and I know that the moment it's out of my mouth. Six weeks ago at this very same table I was begging Bill to go with me to the fertility clinic. It's amazing what modern medical science can do, I insisted, what doctors know these days. He went like a lamb. I cannot imagine the humiliation he had to suffer there in order to indulge my strident faith in medicine; and here I am recanting. But it's the evolutionary imperative, that's what I tell myself, the excuse coming more easily every time I reach for it. If a few inconsistencies, a little manipulation, and even some downright lies, prove to be necessary in order for me to get pregnant, then they will surely be forgiven. The needs of the race trump moral considerations. (Okay, I know that in the wrong hands this could be a dangerous argument, has been a dangerous argument, but mine are not the wrong hands.)

Bill

I CAN'T BELIEVE MY ears. Petra has finally flipped. It's probably the diet. The rice has gummed up her brain. Has she forgotten that fucking clinic? The fucking-clinic. That's how I think of it, literally. It's not a judgment. Not really. I was happy to go, for her sake, that's what I said at the time. I was even prepared to leaf through their magazines, looking at wrinkled pictures of unwrinkled flesh, to coax my reluctant pecker to a mechanical stiffness, a meaningless erection sufficient to pump to the desired outcome. Only, of course, desire had nothing to do with it. I shot into the cup they provided with all the shame of a teenager, but without any of the endorphin rush that used to make the shame worth it. And now she is saying that clinic was all a load of shit.

I take another sip of wine. Anything to avoid returning to the pile of fish and coconut on my plate. Later I will pick myself up a burger. Petra will never know. And so what if she does? I am feeling betrayed now, and dangerous.

Her hands lie on the table beside her food, palms down, pale like two more dead fish, but delicate. Tiny. She has been biting her nails.

"There's two points of view on the whole sodium thing, you know."

"Now, maybe. But before, there was no doubt in your mind. In anybody's."

"I've been onto this website."

"Oh."

"It's research. They have scientific evidence."

"Right. Like stories about some guy who kept a pig's heart alive in a solution of sea salt for fifteen years."

"It was a chicken's heart, for twenty-seven years."

I sometimes think she has forgotten that I trained as a scientist. Biology and Astrophysics. A tough double major. (That was before the landscaping company.) I would be insulted — only the mention of pigs and chickens has made me too hungry to concentrate on anything else.

"It's not the actual salt that's bad for you. It's all the

things they do to it. All the things they add. Did you know there's sugar in most table salt? Sugar!"

"To keep it from clumping."

"And aluminum."

"What about the fact that it's iodized?"

"Exactly. That too."

"Do you have any idea how effective iodization has been in eliminating thyroid disease around the world?"

"Do you have any idea about the increased rates of *hyper*thyroidism since the World Health Organization made that decision?"

I don't have that information at my fingertips, of course, so I can't really argue any further.

Petra

BILL ASKS ME: "ARE we supposed to draw our own sea water in wooden buckets, or can we just dissolve some salt?"

I knew he would give in eventually.

"Not table salt, obviously, since that's suddenly so lethal."

Is he being sarcastic now?

"But sea salt. Can we just dissolve a handful of sea salt in some tap water?"

"Filtered water. It's only a cup a day. Just till we see whether it's effective. And we can test as often as you like." I give him my best dewy-eyed look, pick up a dollop of rice and guide it very slowly between my lips, sucking loudly on my fingers as I remove them. He can always be relied on to like the idea of lots of sex.

"You know, there might be some science behind it, actually, when you think about it."

This is not exactly the response I envisioned, but I am glad he's flexing his brainy scientist muscles. He must welcome any opportunity for that after the last few years of using only the more obvious ones in the landscaping business. I wait for him to go on, looking at him expectantly in the way I imagine he dreams his students might have, the students he never had.

"I remember reading something about dog breeding. They feed the bitch salt to make more puppies in the litter."

Is he pulling my leg? The way he spat the word *bitch*. "Anyway, there are lots of drinks worse that salt water. For fertility, I mean." I am about to tell him about one remedy I read about where you drink a bull's urine that's been collected just after he has copulated, but something in his eyes tells me to leave it alone for now.

Bill

I FIND I DON'T actually mind the taste. We have, in the end, opted for dissolved sea salt rather than actual sea water. Petra, with a little prompting, became worried that there might be other nasty things swimming around in it besides those all-important trace minerals that have allegedly been refined out of table salt. I suspect that it might be just exactly all that teeming life that's supposed to make the potion effective, but I have kept those suspicions to myself. (It's not easy finding a safe spot for dipping water out of the bay, and the strait is a long drive.) Petra flirted with a broad spectrum of possible salts before settling on a winner. Some of the more whimsical candidates — like the one supposed to be coloured by the same micro-organisms that make flamingoes pink — I had to remind her, were not all that closely related to the sea. Not lately, anyway. In the end, we ordered a supply of Le Paludier, a grey salt gathered in Guérande. Neither of us has ever been to Brittany, but the man on the other end of the phone in Montreal assured Petra he was there just last summer and it was very beautiful.

"So what do you think? Pretty good, eh?" She may imagine she has hidden her grimace from me but I catch it. I take another long sip from my glass to make it clear that I expect her to keep drinking too.

"It's kind of weird. Kind of ..."

"Salty? I kind of like it." Now that it's obvious she hates it, I can't resist pushing my advantage. In the week while we waited for the salt to arrive I tried to opt out several times. I told her that surely the treatment was only meant for the woman, intended to make her fruitful like the sea. I even, in a moment of inspiration, pointed out the connection between *la mer* and *la mère*. This had only led to Petra accusing me of being a sexist and not wanting this baby as much as she did. Which baby? I wanted to ask, but did not dare. I swore that I wasn't and that I did and that I was willing to do even stranger things to prove it, if needs be. So now there's something satisfying in the fact that she is finding it harder than I am to drink a glass of salt water.

"Think of it as something else." I take another swig.

"Gross."

"I was going to say caviar." In fact the taste reminds me of the hollow between her breasts on a hot day, the place just above her collarbone, the backs of her knees. Maybe there is something to this after all. I am about to tell her this, to reach over and touch her, when she pads to the sink and pours out what's left in her glass.

Petra

THE COCKY LITTLE FRENCHMAN on the package of salt is laughing at me. Not the retiring servile one who is raking the salt in the background, but the cavalier one with the big hat who stands above and behind the words *Le Paludier* on the label. He is definitely deriding me. To make matters worse, he holds a shield in front of him, emblazoned with some kind of coat of arms. The art is quite primitive, reduced to very basic shapes. On one side of the shield is what looks like the universal sign for the feminine: a circle sits on top of a "t." God knows what it's really meant to represent, in heraldry. On the other side, standing for feathers or plumes or something, are three large comma shapes. Sperm. The promise couldn't be any clearer, but still I cannot bear to drink any more.

Bill claims to like it, which may just be payback, though he is ultimately more adventuresome than I am in some areas. Which leads me to remember how little experience I brought to the relationship when we met, how little inventiveness. Maybe I am not actually meant to reproduce, for all my insistence on the evolutionary imperative. Maybe I am after all just a shy, dry, unsexed bitch who can't even follow through on a resolution to drink a glass of salt water. It was wrong to blame Bill for our failure to conceive. His test came back from the clinic perfectly normal, after all. I simply kept the result to myself, chose to discount it, even though it was my idea to do it in the first place. By then, I was sold on the salt idea and anyway I had come across a webpage on Paracelsus or one of those guys that argued how jerking off, what they used to call "spilling Onan's seed," only produced salt, not real sperm. What Bill had done with those magazines — I am sure there must have been magazines, but he has never wanted to discuss it — therefore simply could not have produced a legitimate sample for study. Now I realize that he has done everything he can. I am the problem.

I turn from the sink, listening to the last burp of the salt water somewhere in the pipes underneath the kitchen, and there is Bill, his tongue rough in the little valley above my collarbone.

Bill

I CAN'T WAIT FOR her to open my gift. All through dinner I have been dropping clever little hints: how the soup was very salty; how I have read that in some restaurants they come around now with a big block of Himalayan salt and grate it right at your table, like Parmesan cheese. She doesn't seem to have paid much attention. It is the most subdued anniversary celebration, although, with only three to compare it to, that may not mean much. The waiter could barely hear her as she ordered, except when he asked her "potato or rice?" "Potato!" she cried as though she were choosing Jesus over Hitler. So much for that diet. That's something, anyway.

It wasn't easy paying for the gift. We both watch the statements pretty closely. I had to salt away little bits of cash each week until I had enough. The man in the antique store was very understanding; he even laughed at my feeble little play on "salting away." I suppose that the market for Georgian saltcellars has all but dried up. Everyone uses shakers; or they don't use anything. The guy is lucky to have found me. To have been found by me.

They were nestled in their box in the front corner of the shop window, next to a set of apostle spoons and half a dozen fish forks. You would have missed them if you didn't know what they were, might have thought they were the matched bases for a pair of cigarette lighters or two no-longer-modish somethings for the dressing table. It was actually the pleated satin of the box's lining that caught my eye. I had just planted a whole bed of petunias exactly that colour. It is a story I can't wait to tell her. I know she'll appreciate the weird mixture of chance and destiny. If only she would cheer up a little.

Petra

I WISH I COULD tell him some other day. The fact that it's our anniversary will make what I have to say seem much more significant than it actually is. More ominous. But I've never been good at not speaking my mind once I have it made up, so today it will have to be. I'll put it off as long as I can though. Why should I spoil his dinner, even though the cook made a good start with that ridiculously salty soup? What I have to say can wait until after dessert, as long as I am not pressed to talk too much before then.

The silly thing is that I know he will probably be fine with it, with what I want to tell him. Even if he is not really fine with it inside, he will pretend for my sake, just like he pretended to want to go to the fertility clinic, just like he gulped down all that salt water. When I say I think we should stop trying so hard, he will most likely just nod and look down, hold my hand for a minute the way he sometimes does, like an old friend at a funeral, then change the subject. He'll be more tentative in his advances in bed, maybe even stop them for a week or two, but I don't think he'll go much longer than that. Then everything will be just as it was before I became obsessed with the stupid Evolutionary Imperative. It just feels so mean to tell him tonight.

When the bill arrives and he has sent the plastic card off to satisfy it, he reaches under his chair and produces a parcel that I haven't seen him put there.

"Open it," he says. "I can't wait any longer."

It is a mess of too-thick corners and tape laid on as if by a child. I feel a hot tear well up and run down my cheek. "I didn't get you … I thought we agreed that the dinner was our present."

"We did. It is. This is just something I *had* to get you. Get *us*. Open it."

The tape and doubled paper finally surrender their treasure. It is a blue box, wooden, covered with what — fabric? Paper? Whatever it is has worn away at the corners. This is not a young box. In the middle of one face is a brass button no larger than a match head. I push it, the lid springs up.

"They're saltcellars. Georgian. Look on the bottoms. The hallmarks are pretty worn, but you can see them with a magnifier. The guy showed me. They have quite a history, you know; saltcellars, I mean, not just these particular ones. In French they were just called *salières* — vessels to hold the salt, but in English we have introduced this little redundancy, you see. Saltcellar is really salt *salière* — salt salt vessel."

"Wow." It is all I can think of to say.

"So why do we call them cellars? Why not just simply 'salters' or something?"

I know the question is rhetorical, make a note to reduce the allowance of minutes on our dial-up internet service.

"It's to emphasize the cellar idea, you see. The 'vessel-ness,' I guess you could say, of where the salt goes. There was this psychoanalyst called Jones. Somebody who knew Freud, and he says that salt stands for —"

But I have stopped listening. I have found the two tiny spoons, their scalloped bowls like delicate flowers on the ends of filament-thin silver stalks.

"Petra, why are you crying? It's the whole fertility thing, you see. I thought you'd —"

"I do. I love them."

Tomorrow will be time enough to tell him what I have decided about trying for a baby. Tomorrow or the next day.

Bill

I WAKE UP AT exactly 2:13 a.m. Atlantic Daylight Time. It isn't the alarm. Petra wouldn't let me set it for that early. When I suggested it last night she just gave me that look she reserves for joggers and street people. As little as two months ago, before we stopped trying to get pregnant after that night I gave her the saltcellars, she had us up at all odd hours of the night, trying to capitalize on a rhythm or a cycle or something. Now, I'm the one who is supposed to be crazy for suggesting we set the alarm for the middle of the night.

"It would be dark, Bill. There would be nothing to see." She was right, of course. Even in Greenwich, where it would be 5:13 and therefore the official start, Universal Time, there would be nothing to see that early. But somehow I wake up on my own — the glowing numbers on the clock confirm it — right at the exact moment of External Ingress: Contact I.

Petra's back is to me; she has thrown off the covers. I gaze across the hills and valleys of her body to where the curtains drift out from the open window. All I am looking for here is a little miracle. All I'm asking for is for the sun to rise and shine in the middle of the night.

"This only happens every 120 years," I said to Petra before we fell asleep. "You'd think we'd at least be allowed to see the whole thing." It isn't strictly speaking true: there will be another chance just eight years from now, but then it will be 112 years after that. And in 2012 the Transit will begin just before sunset, so we'll miss almost all of that from here anyway.

"There will be pictures on the internet," Petra said. As if that were a consolation.

I am sad that she has not shown any enthusiasm about the event. It shows, I think, a kind of laissez-faire attitude to the Universe, and that worries me. "This is an important World Event," I have insisted several times, "A Cosmic Event." Bigger than Afghanistan, or Iraq — bigger even than Palestine or the Olympics. She cares about those things a little, I know that.

I wriggle out of my sticky pyjama pants and prop myself up on my right elbow, watching the white curtains belly and snap in the breeze. And all I can think of is James Cook sailing the salt seas all the way to Tahiti just to watch Venus glide across the face of the sun.

Petra

"I CAN'T BELIEVE I slept through Contact II," Bill groans.

"Internal ingress? I've slept through that plenty of times."

"Not funny Petra. I woke up at exactly 2:13."

"You said."

"But somewhere in there, after that, I fell asleep."

"Until dawn."

"That was always the agreement. We would get up at dawn. 5:29. The radio came on exactly when the sun was supposed to come up. According to the Weather Network that was 5:29. Not a minute earlier."

"It's overcast. Do you want your eggs flipped over or —?" I shiver. My hair is wet from the shower. Bill has said there's no time to dry it; not if I want breakfast, and I do. It's not that I'm all that unhappy to play along with him. It's good to see him taking a lively interest in something. But I do hate it when the droplets find their way past my collar and down between my shoulder blades.

"It might clear up."

"It might." I leave the eggs alone. Hopeful. Sunny side up.

He is polishing the lenses of the binoculars. I am dying to ask him why they have to be so clean if nobody is actually going to be looking through them. I'm not sure he really understands all the stuff he has read about using the binoculars to project an image on a card, though I did go ahead and buy the Bristol board at the drugstore when he asked me to. He has a special filter to use with his camera, too — Aluminized mylar. I had to order that on the internet. It made a welcome substitute for reading about fertility potions.

"I can't help thinking about Janssen this morning," he says as he turns his attention to his telephoto lens. "The revolver thing. Have I told you?"

He has, of course, two or three times. "No."

"This guy Janssen, somebody Janssen, invented what he called a photographic revolver — in 1874 to capture the Transit. It could take forty-eight exposures in seventy-two seconds. Something like that."

"Almost like a movie."

"Only much slower. And on metal plates."

"More like Muybridge maybe." I can see he hasn't heard of Muybridge.

"The idea was to pinpoint the exact moment of contact. They were having a little trouble with that, you see, telling when exactly it was that Venus started on her path across the sun. But with the camera set up it would be easy. It would be one of the images."

I don't point out the obvious fallacies in this line of reasoning. I know how different we are from one another in our conceptions of time and motion.

Bill

WE DRIVE ACROSS THE marsh to the nearest ridge — not really a ridge, but a salt dome. I have scouted it as the optimal viewing site in the area. Besides, I know that Petra likes it here. We used to come for picnics — drawn-out, boozy affairs that usually ended in fucking in the rustling grasses.

"So what would this all look like if we were on Venus?"

she asks as I back the car up the dirt road. There's no-where to turn and I like to know I can get out.

"You aren't really asking that seriously are you?"

"Why not?"

Doesn't she know that a human being landing on Venus would be simultaneously choked, crushed, roasted, and dissolved? Doesn't everybody know that? Was she never a kid? The problem is that I am not sure myself what it *would* actually look like. To a native Venusian. If there were Venusians.

"I guess it would just be business as usual, though, wouldn't it? I mean, if Venus is between us and the sun and if we see her crossing the sun, then she just sees us like always, right?"

I was on the verge of suggesting an eclipse, but of course she is right. I think she is.

The grass is wet, so we spread everything on the warm hood of the car: the binoculars, the Bristol board, the camera, two panes of welder's glass — #14, not easy to come by in town.

"When I was a kid we used old negatives to look through, when there was a solar eclipse. That's not good enough anymore?" She asked that last week too when I came out empty-handed from the third store.

"You can't be too careful. Look at your grandmother's problems."

Petra tried to tell me then how macular degeneration is a common affliction of the elderly, but she still followed me to the next store.

"It never regenerates, you know," I say as I pass her a piece of glass. "Retinal tissue. It doesn't." It's then that I notice the tiny blue crystals that have formed on the buckle of her watchstrap, but I don't comment. She would only laugh if I told her what it is.

"What's so interesting about my wrist?"

I don't know exactly why I take her forearm in my hand then and kiss the pale blue lines that run beneath the milky skin.

"Remember those picnics we used to have?" she says.

I try to get back on task, fumbling with the binoculars and Bristol board.

"Is that a drop of rain?" She asks it gently as one might ask a condemned man if he hears something like a bell tolling somewhere. I can almost believe she cares about seeing the whole thing as much as I do, though I have a hunch it's only that she cares for me. "I saw pictures of Venus once. All those lines are supposed to be salt intrusions, did you know that?"

I do.

"Like what we're standing on right here. A big blister of salt. They think that Venus probably had a salt age like we had an ice age."

I wonder where she has been reading this; am touched that she has wanted to, but a little sorry that it seems to come back to salt again.

"I wonder whether the sky is clear in St. John's." Last week, I mooted the idea of driving there for the event, but she said she'd be sick on the ferry. I hated the idea of standing on Signal Hill with hundreds of science geeks.

"We should have listened to the news. They're probably covering it. Do you want me to turn the car radio on?"

"No point. We're stuck here, aren't we?"

Petra

IT HAS STARTED TO rain and we are sitting in the car. I have not dared to suggest the radio again, but his silence, his disappointment, is killing me. "If we had one of those Raspberry things we could find out how it's going in other places. Maybe see some pictures. Compare notes."

"Blackberries. They're called Blackberries." I know this of course, but am happy to have given him the pleasure of thinking I don't. "That's what the whole thing was about, you know, originally," he says.

"Fruit?"

"Comparing notes. Using parallax to calculate the size of the solar system. People at selected distant observation points, they were all supposed to observe the Transit and then compare notes. It was Halley's idea."

"Kepler's third law comes in somewhere too, doesn't it?" I am not meaning to show off. Just for a minute I actually am quite caught up in it all.

"Is it the third? Maybe."

"It didn't work though," I say.

"Black drop," he mutters.

"Explain that to me again." I am hoping to restore him to his perch as resident expert.

He shakes his head as one might with a particularly slow pupil. "Take your thumb and forefinger and move them as close together as you can without touching."

"I always touch."

"That's okay. Just try. And watch."

"Like this?"

"Exactly. And look, see, just the moment before they touch, look at the shadow, the black. You can't tell that moment from the actual point of contact."

"It was the same with Venus and the sun?"

"Yup."

"And does it work with other things too? This black drop effect? Besides my finger and thumb?"

"Everything. Any time two bodies approach one another that close."

"You can't tell the moment they actually touch."

His lips are tight at first, but I am able to melt them. The rain pelts on the windshield.

Bill

MY WATCH READS 8:05 and 17 seconds as I refasten my belt buckle.

"It is just like on the ads," Petra says as she zips up. "All those cubic litres of cargo space."

Fine for her to say. She didn't have to pull out all the headrests and figure out which bit to fold down first. She didn't have to stand half out in the rain to do all that.

8:05:27, the moment of Contact III, Internal Egress.

"Can we maybe try to imagine it for ourselves?"

I am finally resigned to the possibility that the sky will not clear up. "Okay."

"So, what does it look like now?"

With my finger I draw a circle in the steam on the window.

"That's the sun?"

"Closest we're going to get to it today." Just inside the circle, in the right lower quadrant, I describe a much smaller circle. A dot really. "Venus."

"Right now?"

"Supposedly."

"Then this is one of those special points, a contact — with the black drop thingy. You can't really tell it right to the second, right?"

I wish she would leave the subject alone. 8:05:27 exactly was what the Internet said for third contact. NASA or somebody had said so. That's good enough for me.

"It looks like an olive." She reaches across me to draw a giant martini glass around it. Again I see the watch buckle's tiny blue crystals. Copper sulphate. Salt of Venus. "Or a pregnant belly."

She lies back with her hands folded on her own stomach.

Oh my God. "When?"

"I'm not sure. Not exactly."

"But ..."

"I was late. I bought one of those kits. It turned the right colour."

"But how far along are you?"

"It's not something you can calculate to the day. I mean, unless you don't make love very often."

"We should get you home. Out of the rain."

"I won't dissolve. The car's a pretty good umbrella. Let's see this thing out."

I can't decide whether I love her in that moment more for the new life that is growing inside her or for her willingness to stick to my project. On another window I draw a new diagram of internal egress; adds legs, breasts, and a head. The result is undeniably crude but strangely and primitively powerful. Willendorf.

Petra

I WATCH HIM, HUNCHED over his watch, as he waits for the moment. The tiny hairs that grow out of his ears seem to be concentrating, the scar just below the corner of his eye. His lips move, counting down. I don't try to understand why this event means so much to him. That it does is enough. I stroke my belly, imagine what it will be like when it's huge, like I have swallowed a beach ball. Or a planet.

"8:25:22! External egress!" Seldom has he had an orgasm as loud. "It's over."

Sic transit, I almost say. Instead: "I'm sorry it wasn't … I'm sorry you didn't get to see …"

"It was perfect. Here with you."

I kiss his ear.

"And there's always 2012. There'll be three of us then to watch it."

At least three, I think. But I don't want to frighten him. "Right."

He draws a large circle on the windshield, with a smaller one just outside the lower right part of the circumference. Contact IV. Transit complete. It looks a little like an eyeless clown, but I don't say so.

He starts the car. As the air conditioning kicks in, the drawings fade from view. I think about the Venusians watching us drive across the marsh, over the salt domes, along the dykes, past the sunken forest, home.

Fleur de sel

The guy mowing the lawn has taken his T-shirt off, wrapped it around his head. Martin is reminded of a statue he has seen: Hymen. He watches the bared shoulders as they thrust the lawnmower under a spirea bush. Tiny lithe animals crawl back and forth under the bronzed skin — or reptiles, snakes (a different statue). The man is hot, even though it's only eight-thirty. A half-dozen parallel lines of sweat run down his back and disappear into the waistband of his shorts.

Anneke's mother wanted the grass cut yesterday, but yesterday it rained. So she phoned the company and made them promise for first thing this morning. Anneke's mother always gets results. The mower blade catches on something under the spirea — a root? a rock? — a second's grinding and then a more sustained ringing. The guy looks around quickly to see if anyone has heard, and, satisfied, carries on without even bothering to look under the bush. He does not see Martin. And Mrs. Gleber has gone into town to annoy the florist.

Martin is having trouble determining the guy's age. He's never been good at the quantitative aspects of his profession. Mid-thirties, he thinks. But he doesn't look like the kind of guy you'd expect still to be mowing lawns at thirty-something. His hair is well cut, his shorts are Ralph Lauren; there's none of the expected beer-sag to his belly, he has all his teeth. He smiled at Martin when he first pulled up in his Toyota truck. Either he's a very mature-looking college boy or he owns the company and is shorthanded this morning. Anneke's mother would easily be able to command the owner of the company almost any day, Martin thinks. For this occasion, she could probably get the Pope, especially now with the Bavarian connection.

He decides, though, to back the college-boy hypothesis, thinking about his own students, scattered until September, turning their tender bodies to unaccustomed manual labour. The truck, Martin guesses, belongs to the guy's grandmother. She held on to it blindly against all reason after Grandpa's death, and now it is proving a godsend for the grandson. Martin is proud of his narrative touch.

The guy should have a girlfriend, of course. No, make that several — because he feels it's important not to get tied down too early, and he's been able to find young women who believe the same. They're not sluts or anything, just sensible young women with healthy appetites, and scrupulous hygiene. You can't be too careful about all of that these days. The lawnmower is pointed directly at him now, and Martin looks at the young man's glistening hairless chest and imagines the kissing sounds it makes when it pulls away from his girlfriends' bare tummies. Better, one girlfriend, one torso after all, he revises. He makes the girl a redhead. (Anneke is blond.) The contrast of skin tones is stunning since the young man is dark, olive, Mediterranean somewhere back a bit. They're both drenched in sweat. Dewy. Not from that ridiculously athletic lovemaking you'd see in the movies, though. They've been playing tennis. Martin leaves the young man's shorts on, and gives his girlfriend one of those skirts that is really shorts underneath. He tries running shoes for both, but leaves them only on the young man. His toes need protecting from the lawnmower. Martin can taste the salt on their bodies.

"Martin?"

It's Anneke's father interrupting the story.

"Sir?"

Pause. Martin supposes he is about to be admonished for the hundredth time to call this man *Dad*. Oh god.

"Have the caterers arrived?"

"I haven't seen them. The lawnmower guy is here," he shouts above the roar of the retreating engine.

"That's Bill. He owns the company. He really shouldn't be here. His wife's having some kind of female trouble. My wife can sure make people hop to it when she wants to. Where's Anneke?"

"I don't think I'm supposed to see Anneke this

morning. Superstition. She didn't go to the florist's with her mother — that much I know."

"Probably in her room, then. Fussing. Shout if you see those caterers."

Martin can't remember what Anneke and her mother finally settled on for the food. He bowed out of the process after making the stupid joke about imitating a Roman feast. Salted sow's vulva and teats seemed funnier in his head than when he said the words out loud, especially to his fiancée's mother.

Bill has taken the lawnmower to the far end of the garden. The marquee hides him from sight. Martin tries to rekindle his imagination, but the redhead has fled, and in her place is a blond woman, easily eight months pregnant. That's what Mr. Gleber would mean by female troubles. For a moment, he features the enlarged breasts, the smooth rounded belly, the thin track of fuzz like a pathway below the navel, but this is another man's wife, Martin thinks, Bill's wife, and Martin doesn't do adultery. Not even in his head.

He turns his thoughts to Anneke, imagines her in her room. It's still a version of Barbie's Dream Boudoir, lovingly preserved by her parents through the years of college and graduate school. She was ashamed to show him the room the first time they visited, had refused to let him make love to her in its little canopy bed. It wasn't fear of her parents' hearing them, he knew. After all, Anneke is nearly thirty and even they must accept she is no longer a virgin. Martin pictures her sitting on the puffy little stool in front of the vanity. Anneke is not vain. But there she sits, probably fussing about the blemish, not quite a pimple, that never quite disappears from the side of her nose.

Behind her, on a padded hanger with its head twisted so that it can grip the top edge of the mirrored closet door, is The Dress. It took six weeks of Saturdays to find it. Martin despaired after the third fruitless day, and quipped that he would he happy to marry her stark naked, he loved her that much. Anneke's lips got tight, he had a premonition of salt fish and abstinence, and they made a list of more bridal boutiques to visit.

The bodice is real satin, he knows, surrounded by a cloud of organdy — nylon organdy because it has more body than the real stuff, and doesn't crease. They make it in Japan, which is either a mark of quality or not. When Martin described it to his mother, she told him how her own mother had used salt to stiffen the organdy on *her* wedding dress. "But you didn't see Anneke in the dress, right, Marty?" Martin lied to his mother, said of course not, since it seemed to matter so much to her. He is a good son that way.

In fact, seeing Anneke in the dresses was the compensation, his salary for all of those lost weekends. They had agreed that ancient superstition was not going to stop them from picking out something they both loved. Eyebrows rose at first in most of the shops, until Martin began his critique of the first thing she tried on; then, he figures, most of the clerks took him for the older gay friend.

He really does know clothes. But that was not the real draw. He found there was something unbelievably sexy about sitting around in those sanctuaries of femaleness watching his fiancée try on dresses. And there were the other people's fiancées too, their sock feet incongruous below the cascades of rich white fabrics, black bra straps peeking out from beneath virginal spaghetti, their hair a mess from pulling the gowns on over their heads. He hasn't told Anneke about that part.

The Dress was clearly the hands-down winner the moment she wafted out of the fitting room in it. They both saw that at once. The satin hugs Anneke's hips close as a lover, pushes in on her breasts just enough to make them pout. The organdy obscures, but does not hide, her shoulders, throat, arms. The effect is of Vaseline on the lens; only the darkest freckles whisper through. Her friend Sherry, who is also the maid of honour, has bought Anneke a pair of panties and a bra to match the organdy. Now Martin imagines her before the vanity mirror, trying on the underthings. He is fairly certain that her left nipple shoots him a brown-eyed wink through the gauzy fabric.

The caterers arrive, and he goes to find Anneke's father.

"The caterers are here. Sir." He feels ridiculous; Mr. Gleber is not even ten years older than he is. That is what really makes "Dad" totally out of the question.

"Excellent. Thanks, Martin."

And that is it: a pretty normal interchange between the two of them, actually. Anneke's mother has tried to throw them together by carefully engineered chance a half a dozen times. So they can get to know one another. After the first such time, it was clear they had nothing in common — nothing but Anneke, and Martin is wise enough not to get started on that topic.

They help the caterers unload the van. The head man keeps saying it's not necessary, but Mr. Gleber is adamant.

There are lots of cheeses. Mr. Gleber loves cheese. It is one of the first things that Anneke told Martin about him. He apparently thinks cheeses represent the pinnacle of human achievement.

"It's only milk preserved in salt," Martin had said. (Why couldn't he just let the girl's father enjoy his illusions?)

"That's exactly what my mother says."

At that point, Martin had not met Anneke's mother, but he could sense that she was someone he did not want in his corner, so he had continued: "But what an amazing *idea*, when you think about it — to come up with the idea of pickling milk."

"It's not really pickled, is it?"

"And rennet. How did anybody come up with that? Salting bits of calves' stomachs so you could use them all year round to make the cheese."

"That's gross, Martin."

"Is that what your mother says too?" End of conversation.

Mr. Gleber is lecturing one of the caterer's helpers. "Parmigiano-Reggiano, now that's a patient cheese."

(Martin can't figure out what anyone wants with a huge block of the stuff at a wedding reception. Who will they get to grate it?) "Takes two years for the salt to get to the centre of a wheel of this stuff. Two years."

The young woman smiles ingratiatingly as you might at a raving street person you needed to get around. Martin likes the way her teeth aren't perfectly straight. He'd like to help her, rescue her from his future father-in-law before he starts talking about Pecorino-Romano, but Martin shrivels around Mr. Gleber.

"Two years. That's a long commitment. A lot of waiting for things to ... ripen." He looks at Martin, who wishes he had the nerve to remind the man that Anneke is twenty-nine, and was fully ripened long before she became Martin's research assistant, let alone his fiancée. The young helper sees her chance, rushes away to spread tablecloths. Martin watches the tiny black skirt twitching back and forth and tries to count the hooks on the brassiere through the thin white blouse.

"What's with all the cheese, Mr. G?" It's Sherry, back from a fantastic time in Europe just in time for the wedding. That's what she keeps reminding everyone. She knows the answer, of course — she has known the Glebers forever — but it's the way she is with everyone. Jocular. Desperate to connect. "Hey, Martin."

He thinks about the origins of the tradition of bridesmaids. Anneke has a book; Martin has read most of it. They were to serve as bait to divert marauders from stealing a man's actual bride. Would a marauder make off with Sherry? Would she joke with him till he let her go?

"I've got it, Martin."

"Uh huh."

"Right here. Shall I show you? Do you want to see it?"

"Um. Sure." Martin has no idea what the "it" is, but he is reasonably confident that Sherry does not plan to reveal a body part, not with Mr. Gleber ten feet away. Besides, he has seen all of the secret places of Sherry's body before. A year before he saw Anneke's, as it happens. It was one of those episodes that get teachers fired; he's still mystified over how he had let it happen. Something about being able to resist everything except temptation. Who said that?

The ring is white gold. "*Weisse geld*," whispers Sherry, who can't seem to shake off Europe, or wants it to look that way. "That's also what they call salt in Berchtesgaden, did you know that? *Weisse geld*."

The band is thinner than Martin would have chosen for himself, but Anneke was determined that she should pick it out. "It's a token of *my* love for *you*," she said. "It wouldn't be the same if you picked it out." He will learn to like it, he tells himself.

"It's beautiful, isn't it?"

"It's very plain," Sherry announces. Martin wonders whether she is a little jealous. He doesn't like to flatter himself, but Sherry did sleep with him first. He tried to tell Anneke about it once, fearful that Sherry might otherwise beat him to it, but she had become bogged down in the parable he was using, and never actually got the message behind it. It is a problem he often has when he's giving lectures too: his students get stuck on the medium and never grasp the message. This parable was a favourite: the Hopi salt-woman.

"The Twins' grandmother, the Spider-woman," he had begun, "was buried nude in a trench."

"Why?"

"She couldn't keep up."

"So they buried her alive?" Anneke was already veering off course.

"That's not the point."

"It must have been pretty much the point for her, though."

"It was to punish the Hopi, not her."

"What had they done?"

"For starters, they hadn't invited the Twins to join their dance. They didn't think they were clean."

"Anybody who treats their grandmother like —"

"They always wiped their noses on the backs of their hands."

"Gross."

"It came in handy, as it turned out."

"Handy?"

"See, finally one young Hopi woman did invite the Twins. There was stew. But no salt. The Hopi didn't know about salt in those days. So the Twins just —"

"Oh Jesus. That's completely disgusting."

"That's what the Hopi thought. They said they would

never invite the Twins back. So the Twins turned the Hopi to stones."

"Forever?"

"No, just for a while."

"Well, how long?"

At this point he had given up. He never got to the part of the story that really mattered: how the Hopi men had to have sex with the Twins' buried grandmother in order to get access to the salt mine, because now it turned out that they had actually developed a taste for salt. Sherry was the old Spider-woman, he wanted to tell Anneke, while she, Anneke, was the salt mine. He had had to sleep with Sherry to make his way to Anneke. It maybe wasn't the greatest analogy, on reflection.

"What if I were to get the ring stuck on my finger?" Sherry asks. "Or my thumb, more likely. Jeez, you have big fingers Martin."

"Maybe you should put it back in the box."

"Are you afraid? Would we be bound forever?"

Martin wishes that Mr. Gleber had not sidled away.

"Relax. It only works for the ring finger. It's the vein, you know, the vein from that finger that runs straight to the heart. *Vena amoris*, it's called, did you know that? Of course you did. You know all that kind of stuff. I don't know where the vein from the thumb goes. The big toe, probably." Sherry admires her own big toenail, a defiant cherry glistening with two drops of dew from the lawn. Martin remembers sucking that toe, and he prays the marauders will show up soon.

"Do you see this stuff?" It's Mr. Gleber, not a marauder come to abduct Sherry.

"Moth crystals?" asks Sherry. At least she's distracted.

"It's supposed to be salt, the caterers say. God. You could almost use it on the roads in the winter."

"It's called fleur de sel," Martin explains. "A delicacy."

"You mean you know about it?"

"We asked them to supply it for us. It's very hard to find around here."

"It'd never come out of a shaker. Is that Bill cutting the grass?" And Sherry slips away.

"My daughter actually eats this stuff?"

"We both do, when we can."

"She didn't learn that in this house. Mrs. Gleber's death on sodium."

"It's French. Well, obviously, with the name, but ..."

"And you just shovel it onto your food?"

"It's a delicacy."

"You said."

"The crystals form on the surface of evaporation pools when there's a certain wind. A hot, dry wind. Only the women salt-workers are allowed to harvest them. It's very delicate work, takes a special touch. Makes it precious. Try a flake."

"Without anything to put it on? Who does that?" But Mr. Gleber does touch a crystal to the end of his tongue. "Tastes like salt. What does it cost? We've got a hundred and fifty people are going to eat here tonight. How much salt is that?"

"This isn't for eating."

"But you said you …"

"Oh we do, when we can, but we wouldn't dream of feeding it to all those people tonight."

"What do you mean 'those people'?" Martin sees an artery throb on Mr. Gleber's neck.

"It's for our pockets, Anneke's shoes maybe."

"Her shoes?"

"A custom. To ensure …"

"Whose custom? Don't you ever stop being a professor? Ensure what?"

"Fertility, actually. To be fair, it's not really an actual custom of any one group in particular. It's more a sort of an amalgam we've made up, I guess you could say. In some parts of England they actually smash a plate of salt on the groom's head."

"I can see why you decided not to go with that one. Just don't tell my wife all this, okay? Salt and fertility — who the hell knew?"

Martin is on the verge of launching into his party piece on the old superstition that mice can reproduce in salt without benefit of sex, but he checks himself when he can't think of a usable euphemism for sex.

"So, you should probably hang on to this then." Cheeks burning, the older man passes Martin the little cardboard cylinder of salt, makes an excuse about paying Bill, and flees down the garden after Sherry.

Martin sits on a wrought-iron chair, dabs his forefinger with his tongue, and sticks it in the jar. He gazes at the crystal that sticks to his fingertip, sees a French peasant woman, skirts hiked above her knees, wading at the edge of an evaporation pond. The water is blood-red, the sign of supersaturation. A hot dry wind tickles a tendril of hair that wisps down the back of her neck. She leans forward to skim off the fleurs; and then he realizes that he has no idea what they use for that job. Is it some kind of net? Their hands? Obviously not the clumsy rakes the men use. He eats the flake of salt, dips his finger and eats another, hoping for enlightenment.

"It's not good for you, you know," says Sherry, her breath hot and dry behind his ear.

"The jury's still out. You do need a certain amount. Your body —"

"It's only a desire that's interpreted as a need."

"Ernest Jones." Martin is tickled that Sherry remembers this.

"Somebody like that, probably. Who can be bothered to keep them all straight?"

"Try a flake."

"What if I can't stop?"

"I'll put the lid on."

"After I've turned into a pillar of salt. No, I don't think so."

Martin does not tell her that he pictures her more as one of Lot's daughters than his wife, although quickly he wishes he had said something to take control of the conversation because she suddenly blurts out, "Semen's salty."

"Jesus, Sherry." Pause. "Is it?"

"Of course. You don't mean you've never tasted ..."

He remembers now why he had not pursued their relationship. He remembers too the sticky pool on his belly last night in the motel room. A desire rationalized as a need.

"Ask Anneke."

He won't.

"God, Marty, ask *anyone*."

He would run if he could, straight to Anneke. Not to ask about that, but for protection from this harpy. But it could be bad luck. On their wedding day. And not entirely fair: it was Sherry, not Anneke, he had been thinking about last night alone in his hotel room. A harmless infidelity, to be sure, but arguably an infidelity nonetheless.

"Your ears can get redder than anyone I know."

"Maybe it's all the salt. Blood pressure."

"Maybe. It's cute. Charming."

Martin thinks she is about to kiss him. Mr. Gleber arrives a minute too soon.

"Martin, I don't think you've met Bill."

"My hand's a little grubby," says Bill. You don't want to smell of gas on your wedding day." Martin pulls his right hand back and pockets it. "Congratulations."

"That's what they always say to the groom isn't it? Congratulations, like you've won something or done something." Sherry takes a pinch of salt and drops it on the tip of her outstretched tongue. "And what is it for the bride? I wish you every happiness? Like there's some kind of doubt." The salt hits the back of her throat and she splutters.

"You'd better get home to check on that wife of yours, and get yourself cleaned up, Bill. We'll see you tonight?"

"I wouldn't miss it. I don't know about Petra yet." And Bill turns and walks back down the lawn to fetch his mower, his shirt still tied around his head like Hymen's veil. Martin can almost taste the tang of sweat on his back.

And then suddenly Anneke is there.

"Honey-pie, what are you doing? Martin's not supposed to see ..."

"It's all right, Daddy. Martin and I don't believe all that mumbo-jumbo."

Martin waits for somebody to make an anthropologist joke.

"What's the matter, sweetie?" Sherry puts her arm around Anneke's neck and kisses her cheek. They can all see she has been crying.

"I just need a minute or two with Martin."

"Baby, it's normal to get the jitters. It's a big step. Your mother and I —"

"It's okay, Daddy, the caterers can keep on working. It's not that."

"C'mon Mr. G, let's go see how that wheel of Parmesan is doing." The bridesmaid spirits the bride's father away. Martin is not sure he wants to be left alone with his bride-to-be. The tears are streaming down her face now.

"I wanted this day to be perfect."

"It will be," he says. "It is."

"Rotten fucking timing."

Has she found someone else? Bill, perhaps, his conjugal advances frustrated by his pregnant wife?

"I counted so carefully."

"What?"

"My period, goddammit, my stupid period. I thought —"

"Is that all?"

"But it ruins our wedding night. I wanted it to be special, I —"

"You're curing in salt."

"What?"

"That's what they call it in some parts of France: to have your period is to be curing in salt."

"That's just great."

"They say you're *en salaison*. They'd keep you away from the yeast."

"Martin, this is serious —"

"But apart from that, it's considered very lucky."

"Lucky?"

"For a wedding night. Especially lucky. A great portent."

"It is?"

"Sure." He pulls her to him, kisses the tears from her rimy face. Then he passes her the jar of fleur de sel. "For your pockets."

"I'm not going to do the shoe, is that okay? I think it might be uncomfortable."

"Of course."

"I love you, Martin. And thank you, you know, about the French thing."

"I love you."

He is pretty sure she'll never find out how much he made up.

Proserpina

The queue at the head of the wooden slide is dwin-
dling fast. Sherry has worked out that there should
be time for her to go down by the stairs as long as she
starts before this line is half gone. But having watched
fully two-thirds of the tourists make the plunge, she
has continued to hover, head light, bowels burning, torn
between terror of the slide and dread of embarrassment.
The stairs have been stigmatized by their guide as being
for the "faint-of-heart" (she thinks that is the right
translation), and she wants everyone (especially him)
to know she is not that. So she stands and watches as her
black-suited companions from the train, counted off
in groups of *ein-zwei-drei*, are instructed to straddle
the twin rails of blond wood, lift their feet, and let go: the
quickest way into the depths of the mine; the traditional
way into the *salzbergwerk* for centuries. She starts for
the stairs. Makes a rapid estimate. Reaffirms what she

already knows: there is no way she can go down that way now and still stay with the tour.

A skittish-looking man tries to dig in his heels just as the guide gives him a hardy shove on the shoulder to start his descent. There is a blue streak of German from the guide. Sherry recalls that the German word for guide is *führer*. The scolded man bows his head, raises his sneakers, and his group of three whooshes down into the mine. Sherry thinks she recognizes him as the man in front of her on the train. He looks like it from the back, anyway, which is all you can know from the ride into the mine. She shivers, remembering the forced intimacy of the little train: how you mounted the bench and wrapped your knees around the stranger in front. You bought your ticket in the pavilion on the surface. It told you the time you might start your tour. Only when it was your appointed moment would the electronic turnstile accept your ticket and allow you in. Going the old program one better, Sherry thought: making sure the people run on time for the trains. The changing-rooms were first. Gargantuan women behind counters sized you up with a glance and shoved bundles of coarse black cloth across at you. There was an oddly shaped belt to hold the trousers up. At least that's what Sherry supposed at first. Or was it to secure the jacket? She thought of Alice with Humpty Dumpty. A woman on the tour explained in broken English and many gestures that it was actually to protect the kidneys from the cold. Sherry nodded her understanding, though she couldn't really see how.

Once dressed in what the placards along the corridors assured them was traditional miner's gear, the masses of now-identical tourists were herded to a platform where they waited for a place on the train. Sherry wondered whether anyone had considered shaving heads to complete the picture.

The guide is gesturing to her. It's time, come here, something like that. She and he are the only ones left at the top of the slide. It is unavoidable. She knows that the train has already vanished back through the tunnel to take on its next group of fantasy-miners. Surely she will be safe going down with the guide. He must have done it thousands of times before.

She would rather be the one in back, but she supposes that it is against the rules. He must be the last man down. Like a captain with his ship. Is that right? His hands closing on her waist make her jump at first. Even through the multiple layers of clothes — her own, the costume — she feels ticklish there; she always does. He smells of beer and garlic. His pelvis grinds into her buttocks as he pushes off.

For the first second or two, Sherry thinks this is not so bad, I can do this, what was I frightened of? But then thought becomes an impossibility. Her womb displaces her stomach, her stomach pushes her heart against her ribcage. Her head throbs. Something flashes.

They stop, and the guide is helping her up. She thinks his hand rests longer than necessary on her waist. She hopes she has not screamed out loud.

Everyone is laughing. The skittish man is pointing to the camera mounted on the rock ceiling above the slide and is mugging a series of frightened faces one after another, like snapshots. The guide moves off to the far end of the group. Sherry watches his retreating buttocks and remembers a statue. Where was it? The Mirabell Gardens, she decides. Salzburg. Two days ago. Pluto and Proserpina, she divined, though she could not be certain — the official guidebook for the gardens cost five euros. Both naked, she thinks, except for Pluto's crown — a laughably unnecessary footnote to his unmistakably regal behind.

The guide — Kurt, he said his name is — wears no crown. Only the silly little hat that goes with his uniform. For he is in uniform, furthering the grim illusion she has had before, when people were being herded on his train, of history repeating itself. It's black wool, by the look and feel, with white cord trim and brassy buttons, shiny boots, all topped with a pillbox draped in gold braid and crested by a huge plume. Sherry feels sorry for him, being made to parade around in that ridiculous getup. By his build she knows he could be a real miner, working somewhere in an adjacent shaft, pummelling the hazelnut rock with an enormous machine until it gives up its salt. Instead, he helps tourists down slides, grins for photos, and begs for tips at the tour's end, filling his hat with tiny salt shakers so that you will take one out and drop a coin in its place.

There are listening stations for this part of the tour. Sherry finds the one labelled "GB," proud not to make the mistake of some of her English-speaking peers in the group who choose "E" and end up listening to Spanish. She watches Kurt's lips move and tries to concentrate on the sounds coming from the speaker over her head. It is not possible to block the sound of Kurt's voice entirely, and the result is a kind of palimpsest, but she is able to glean the gist. This is the König-Ludwig *grotte*. Luminous rocks, a succession of carefully crafted arches. A kind of shrine — she can't tell whether to King Ludwig or to his God. Sherry thinks about St. Barbara, made patroness of miners by virtue of her association with thunder and fire. But the thunder and fire came after, directed at her father, after he had beheaded her for being a Christian. It wasn't anything to do with Barbara at all.

Someone in the English group standing near the Spanish loudspeaker asks whether slaves were ever used to do the work here in Berchtesgaden, as was the case in some of the great Polish salt mines. Kurt looks blank. A tall young man with German clothes and a North American face tries to translate. Kurt colours a little and shrugs — universal signal for "I may know, but I will not say." He hurries the group on.

Sherry is at the back of the group so she cannot make out the guide's words as he recedes down a tunnel, even if she were able to understand them. Instead, she overhears the tall young man explaining to a woman who might be his mother the real significance of the little chapel carved out of the rock. It goes back to the Celts, he says, who believed that prayers uttered in a salt mine were sooner heard by the gods. Sherry hangs back then, after the others have joined the end of the line, and whispers a few words of her own.

There is a large underground lake: very concentrated brine, judging from the grimaces of those who are taking Kurt up on his invitation to taste. They are all herded onto a barge. Sherry likes water even less than slides. She focuses on the large sign affixed to the rock face at the far end of the lake: "*Glück auf!*" it reads. Some of the English-speaking people on the tour are having fun with homophony. "*Glück auf!*" they playfully snarl at one another, sometimes raising a middle finger in concert. "Happy out," she corrects them mentally, marvelling at the mix of humour and sobriety, hope and acceptance, in the traditional miners' salutation. Only for an instant does she allow her eyes to drift to Kurt, who stands joking at the front of the barge, a cheerful Charon ferrying them all across the Styx.

She thinks about how quiet he was, by contrast, how stealthy, the first time, while they had sat and watched the video. On the screen, a tanned and fit middle-aged man posed in front of rank upon rank of sparkling vats and machines two or three storeys in height — the *neue saline* at Bad Reichenhall, a subtitle reported — and he droned on about the importance of the salt industry to the economy of Bavaria. "*Die weisse geld!*" he kept crowing at the end of each segment, drowning out the droning translation on Sherry's headphones. The thesis of the video was exclusivity: the rarity of salt, its position as a precious commodity over the span of recorded history, even the exclusiveness of the tours of the mines in centuries past. Sherry had wondered whether Hitler brought his pals down for the tour when things got dull on the Kehlstein or wherever. She also wondered whether the narrator knew much geology, or that you could find salt almost anywhere.

At first she had thought that, in the dark, Kurt's hand must have mistaken her thigh for his own. Even when his hand moved higher she held to that theory. Only when he began to try to find a way between the heavy cotton trousers and her tunic, bypassing the belt, had she been certain that what he was doing was conscious: their uniforms were so unmistakably different. The video flashed images of the very mine they were in, the drone continued about *sinkwerks* and brine canals and *wildwasser*. Sherry gasped. She did not yell. Her hands stayed limp, two dead herrings at her sides. By the time the lights had come up, the guide had taken up his position at the front of the room, ready to lead them all through the *salzmuseum*.

After the lake there are the breathing shafts. These are what drew Sherry to the mine in the first place — the promise of help with her asthma. As it turned out, the curative salt-mine tunnel, featured in glossy promotional photographs with a prettily lit pool and dozens of neatly arranged deck chairs, proved to be a distinct and expensive transaction, to be conducted separately at another ticket booth. It was not part of the regular tour, and it was more than Sherry could afford. She has had to settle for the few whiffs of the magic air from the top of the breathing shafts.

Most of the people on Sherry's tour pause briefly to suck in a draft from the shafts. Several laugh and shake their heads as they exhale, as if they are passing a joint. One man beats on his chest like Tarzan to demonstrate his newfound healthiness. Sherry suffers a sympathetic wheeze when she sees this assault, which triggers more wheezes. A German couple and the tall young man and his mother all linger longer to breathe the salt-laden air. Sherry imagines that none of them can afford the special trip to the curative salt-mine tunnel either. "Asthma?" the German woman asks her. She pronounces it as three syllables evenly. Sherry nods and smiles, losing the breath she has been holding in, and beginning to cough. This sets the others off and they, hacking, all hurry along the tunnel to catch up.

All but Sherry look disappointed to discover that the next stop is the video screening room. They settle onto the padded forms like benched athletes, wearily putting on the headphones where needed, and staring straight ahead at the screen. Sherry is not going to bother with the phones at first, but then she thinks better of it: everything must be the same as it was the day before. If history is going to repeat itself. Perhaps Kurt would never have tried if she had not been cocooned in her own sonic envelope of bored English translating enthusiastic

German. The room goes dark. The video starts. Sherry waits. The tanned man talks about *die weisse geld* and develops his thesis on exclusivity. Kurt stays where he is at the front of the room. She can see him in the glow from the screen. Is he looking for her? She sits in exactly the same place as yesterday. There is an empty seat beside her, just as there was then. The only difference is in what she has chosen to wear under the heavy cotton pants and tunic. But he cannot know this.

As the narration pushes on into *sinkwerks* and brine canals and rock-smashing, she realizes that Kurt will not be coming to sit beside her. She replays the events of the day before. How he was back in his place at the front of the room when the lights came up, but how he almost certainly smiled at her later in the *salzmuseum*. And how, when she lifted the tiny cylinder of salt from his hat at the end of the tour and dropped a few coins in in its place, his hand seemed to quiver. She took the tiny sample of salt back to her hotel and placed it beside the other souvenirs she had lined up on the dresser, but later she carried it with her to the dining room, where she sprinkled it liberally on her schnitzel. It was her pomegranate, she thought, the thing she has eaten from the underworld. And that was when she had known that she must go back down to him.

She is the first through the *salzmuseum*, though nobody lingers long, and she is the first to take a tiny salt from his hat, working her fingers so as to give the illusion that she is depositing money in its place. As she looks up, Kurt is gazing straight into her eyes.

"Morgen," he says.

"Tomorrow," she thinks.

Holy Water

It is performed in one clean continuous movement down and up again. Two women executing a tango, Peter thinks, as long as you overlook the sputtering that follows the dip, the rat-tails plastered to the eyes. But then he reminds himself that this is exactly why they are gathered by the water's edge today: for the inconvenience, the discomfort, the danger.

The women, their dance complete, embrace and part. The deaconess reaches to brush the hair from the other woman's eyes, a lover saying goodbye, before she passes her on to Deacon Paul who leads her back towards the beach.

"Last year, we weren't allowed to baptize in the lake," Julie told him one night. It was about six weeks after they had begun seeing one another. "The E. coli scare, you remember?" They were in the bath. She had pinched her nose then, hiked her knees, slid her bottom along the tub floor, disappearing for a few seconds beneath the soapy water. When she surfaced, her golden hair was slicked back from her face and lay flat behind her ears. She opened her lids and smiled. (It was a professional thing. He sometimes tried the same trick when he lectured.) "You can't imagine how terrible that was."

"Nobody could be baptized?" He loved how they could carry on a theological conversation at the same time he was watching the droplets run down her breasts, pause for breath at the nipples, and fall into the bathwater below. It was a marriage between the spirit and the flesh he had thought was reserved for medieval popes.

"People have been being baptized at our church for way more than two-hundred years." It is a Planter church. Peter isn't sure who the Planters were or what they are supposed to have planted, but he always professes awe. "We couldn't just stop cold turkey."

"Couldn't you go up to the strait, do it in the ocean? No E. coli there."

"The water has to be fresh."

Peter remembered the faint tang of salt in the water that stood by the door of his childhood church. He had tasted it once, though he had been told not to. "What did you do?"

"We used the Constantine's swimming pool."

When Peter made a joke about the pool-cleaning robot sucking away loudly while Satan was being cast out, Julie stood up, stepped from the bath and wrapped herself in a huge towel. In those early days, he had not taken the whole thing entirely seriously. He had not been able to fathom how she did, how she could, naked in the tub.

He knows the water tests have come back negative this year — which actually means that the Department of Health is positive that there is no danger. Julie fretted about it through most of the spring. The outdoor baptismal service is the high point of her year; and this year, she says, it means even more to her because of his commitment. In what he intended as the ultimate vote of confidence during the darkest days of her worrying he actually vowed to go through with the ceremony in the murky lake regardless of what the tests found.

"It's supposed to be about danger, isn't it?" he had said. "In its origins? The threat of drowning and all that?" He had learned by then not to go on about ancient Greek Mysteries and Hebrew baptismal practices. She gets edgy, doesn't like to be compared. "What's a little E. coli?" He is proud of this gift he has made her of his faith, this unequivocal statement of his conviction. And he tries not to be bothered that she has not for a moment tried to talk him out of it.

The newly baptized woman is being handed her glasses and a towel. It is one of those swirled sundaes of day-glo flowers that can be seen languishing in the window of the local department store all summer long, begging to be taken to the beach. She is weeping, her shoulders heaving. For a moment, Peter thinks she may go into some kind of rapture.

"The gift of tongues," Julie has told them all in an

early class, "is just exactly that: a gift. If you hope for it at your baptism you will, most likely, be disappointed. The Lord will give it to you at a time and place He sees fit, if He sees fit. Baptism is a big step towards grace; but there is always more work to be done."

Some of Peter's classmates had looked downcast at this news. One even dropped out. They heard later he was starting his own church somewhere in rural Nova Scotia. Peter, on the other hand, had to struggle to hide his relief. He loved Julie, but he had been raised Catholic in an era when you could, and did, do plenty with tongues, but speaking in them wasn't yet on the regular menu.

The woman's sobs dissolve into laughter. She shivers and turns her attention to the lake. She will not receive the gift today. The Holy Spirit has once again resisted the temptation to show off.

Disappointed, the bystanders cast their eyes elsewhere in search of a sign, but Peter continues to gaze at the woman. The men are allowed to wear T-shirts and pants, but the women still wear the more traditional white robes. Peter can see sections of her bathing suit through the gown where it clings to her body. He can't help imagining the body beneath the bathing suit then: the round belly, the full breasts, the newly baptized bush. It's the solstice that's to blame, he decides: the female earth energies are at their height. Around Julie, he has to be careful to suppress his habit of analyzing everything as an anthropologist. Early in the month, too early, after a bracing swim in the strait, they had stood on the empty beach, bathing suits crusted in sand at their feet, making goose-pimpled, purple-skinned love, teeth chattering, threatening to sever their tongues. Afterwards, she had wondered what they had been doing, what they could have been thinking, and he had told her it was a kind of fertility rite, an affirmation of the life force. "You were Aphrodite, coming out of the waves," he had said. "We were, you know, subject to a higher power." It seemed like the right thing to say. She said she wanted to go home and have a shower, she couldn't stand the way the salt prickled on her skin like guilt.

He had forgotten how easily guilt trumps fertility, and fresh water rinses away salt.

A SECOND CANDIDATE IS wading into the water now, steered at the elbow by Deacon Paul. She is a bit of a special case, younger than the usual — only twelve, Julie told him a week ago.

"Aren't they supposed to be of an age when they can make decisions for themselves? Isn't that the crux of the whole debate?" was his response.

"It's her parents' idea."

"You mean *they* decided to make the decision *for* her?"

"You sound like it's a punishment, a bad thing. Her parents think it might help her, that's all."

"Help her?"

"She can be a little wild, a little, um, unmanageable. They think that if the Spirit could tame her —"

"Now you're the one making it sound like a punishment."

They had been camping at the time. Peter had bought one of those trailers that perch on the bed of a pickup truck, but after the discussion Julie pitched for herself a pup tent that he had not even seen her pack.

The little girl has turned back to face the shore. Deacon Paul is leaning over her, saying something Peter can't hear. It is no doubt something reassuring. Julie is obviously trying to remain placid, waiting in the choco-late water, half turned away. I am not worthy to unloose the latchets, he thinks. There is a flurry in the crowd near Peter, and the girl's mother strides to the water's edge.

Peter tries to remember back to when he was twelve and how he would have spent this day. It would have been long before he knew to call it St. John's Eve, but it had always been special. School was just out. They had bonfires, burned their books — some of them already in training to sit on school boards. Without knowing why, they lit their fires as people had been doing that same day for centuries to relieve sickness in cattle, to ensure fertility of the grain, to show the sun that they too knew how to shine. Surely this girl would rather be at a bonfire than standing in the chilly water, repenting her sins. How many could she have committed in her short life?

The mother has waded in past her knees, sacrificing a brand-new pantsuit. She and Deacon Paul are bent over the girl from either side, two angels from a medieval painting. The girl nods. Peter can tell she is crying, trying to catch her breath, but the nod is all the adults need. Mother, deacon, and daughter all turn and head into the lake.

Julie's robe has floated up to form a lily pad around her. Peter suddenly remembers the weights. There were small lead sinkers he was supposed to remind her to baste back into the hem of the robe after it had been through the wash. It was his idea to take them out. He had told her they would wreck his machine, and handed her the seam-ripper. He imagines her now as the fishes must see her — a reluctant Marilyn Monroe, her skirt drifting above her waist, buoyant as if in brine.

Utterly unbelievably, she doesn't know Marilyn Monroe. The name came up one night when they were talking about the Great Loves of History, a conversation he was more interested in than she was. He had tried to explain, but the best he had been able to manage was an analogy with Madonna circa 1986. Arthur Miller, Joe DiMaggio, even J.F.K., rang no bells with Julie.

Another time he had tried Strindberg on her — because of her name. She had never seen *Miss Julie*, and he realized how even the beheaded canary seemed pale, contrived, when you just told the story. Julie did rise to the occasion enough to see an allusion he had never pondered: "Like Salome and John the Baptist." "I guess," he had replied, "only the head's on a cutting board, not a platter." Strindberg set the play on St. John's Eve, he remembers now.

The trio has reached the waiting priestess. The little girl is up to her armpits in the water, and the hem of Julie's flowing gown reaches out to her, ripples along the small mounds where proper breasts will someday sprout. She whispers something to the girl that is probably not about breasts. The girl smiles. Then, in a voice much louder and deeper than she used for the first candidate, she asks "What is your name?"

Is she shouting, Peter wonders, to compensate for the vulnerability she must be feeling, defrocked beneath the surface of the water in her white Speedo? Or have the parents succeeded in persuading her that Satan is hard of hearing, burrowed deep in his stronghold within this child?

The girl must manage to utter her name, though too quietly for Peter to hear, because Julie goes on: "Have you repented towards God?"

Again the response is too low for Peter to make it out, but from the change in the mother's body language it is clear the answer is yes.

"I now baptize you in the name of Jesus Christ for the remission of your sins."

Julie's gown gets in the way, but the dip is still quite smooth and very quick. The emergent girl doesn't appear to know that anything has even happened. Peter wonders whether she will remember as little of this as he remembers about his own baptism, the first one. There are photographs in a binder, of course, snapshots of him as a tiny puddle of unselfconscious flesh, lying on his tummy wearing an heirloom-brocaded dress.

Once, a few weeks ago, he managed to bring the subject up, briefly. "I would probably have just been sprinkled the first time, right?" He did not add that the water would have been a little salty. Nor did he mention the pinch of salt he knew had been put between his lips. *Sal sapientiae.* That was the practice before Vatican II — long enough ago that she was not likely to have heard of it. "Or do they pour the water? What's that called?"

"Affusion. They call it affusion, pouring."

"And dunking's immersion, I know that. So what's sprinkling? I think I was probably just sprinkled. That hardly counts, does it?"

"It's mostly Anglicans who are sprinkled, I think."

"My father was Anglican before he converted to Rome for my mother. And then we kind of drifted back."

"Infant baptism is wasted on persons who are too young to take on the responsibility."

He wanted to tell her to try to sell that line in the first circle of Dante's Inferno, but he had long since made up his mind to lead a new life. Instead, then: "And think how terrifying it must be, being handed over to a stranger who splashes water on your face."

"The terror is a rightful part of it. The discomfort. But it's for older people, people who make a commitment by facing the fear."

"I love the water. Is that going to be a handicap?"

"Nobody doubts your commitment to the Lord, Peter."

That was the moment when he should have asked her

to go over one more time the definition of idolatry. That was when he should have asked if it was all right that he had trouble distinguishing his love of the Lord from his adoration of her, the Lord's deaconess. But her praise of his commitment was a kind of aphrodisiac for them, and they moved on to other things.

He has not invited his parents to see him baptized. "Who wants to see a grown man dunked under the water to accomplish what was already done for him perfectly well and far more tastefully when he was a baby?" That would be his mother. "What, watch a rerun?" his father would say. Julie was upset when he said he wasn't asking them to come. "This will be the most important day of your Christian life," she said. "They should be here to share it." Then: "Are you ashamed to have them meet me?"

"They would love you. I love you."

She subsided, and his parents' not coming became a kind of shared burden between them, a betrayal of love by two people who were never even asked.

In fact, Peter was not sure that his parents would even like Julie. He is not sure they will actually still love him now that he is to be totally immersed. They are salt-water types, sprinklers after all, he has decided, from generations of sprinklers and pourers. Sprinkling, Julie told him when he begged her, is called "aspersion."

THE GIRL AND HER mother are drying off on the beach. The congregation has retreated a little to give them room. Their shadows are short, even this early in the day. Peter

is reminded of Stonehenge. It was '83 or maybe '84 —
before it was closed, before it was opened up again. Watching the sun come up over the heel stone, like a druid, is
another experience he has edited for Julie's sake. It was
part of another phase he has kept from her. Because
that's what lovers do. They give things up for one another.
He has loved making her these mute presents of sacri-
fice, these silent erasures of his past.

It is Peter's turn now. Deacon Paul is beckoning.
Julie has turned away again. There is a block of ice in his
stomach. It could be worse, he reminds himself. It's not
like it's the cult of Cybele and Attis — he's not a eunuch
about to be baptized in bull's blood. This reassurance
gets him as far as the water's edge. He turns to look at
the twelve-year-old initiate. Does she wink?

Deacon Paul's hand is cold and wet when he takes it.
"Peter." "Paul." Peter thinks that Deacon Paul doesn't
like him much. He thinks Deacon Paul likes Julie a lot.
Probably loves her. Is jealous. This gets him into the
water.

There are mussels; they cut his feet. Why has he been
too vain to wear the dumb little aqua sox Julie bought
him at Canadian Tire? Or his Tevas? Deacon Paul has
Tevas on.

The water is colder than he expected. Maybe his feet
will go numb and take away the sting of the cuts. He
imagines the blood clouds wafting up through the water
with every step, and the mud — Jesus, those tests had
better be accurate — sifting into the open wounds.

He has disinfectant in the camper. Afterwards, he'll sprinkle it all over his feet. There should be enough left. He used some when he ripped his palm on a nail one day, and Julie needed a little when she cut herself slicing the tomatoes for sandwiches last Saturday. They were camping at the beach, the real beach, salt water, not the edge of this shallow pond. In the morning it was easy for him to believe the ocean that lay spread before them was formed of the gods' tears, or Persephone's. He could not remember which it was supposed to be. But this was not something he could say to Julie, whose patience with the salt water appeared nearly exhausted. The knife she was using was so sharp she had not noticed the wound until the tomatoes were stewed in blood. He had been the one to cry out. Then he had taken her wounded finger into his mouth. She tasted of salt and rust.

"What are you doing?"

"I don't know.'"

"I think I need some disinfectant, Peter."

But he really did know. There are two sacraments. Baptism and the Supper of the Lord. What meanest thou by this word *Sacrament*? Answer: I mean an outward and visible sign of an inward and spiritual grace. Blood.

They rinsed the tomatoes and ate them. The bread sopped up the extra water. He was sure he could taste the salt of her still.

"In Sardinia, we ate tomato sandwiches with basil leaves all drizzled over with olive oil."

"When were you in Sardinia?"

"I told you, didn't I?" But of course he had not. It had been late in May a dozen years before, at the peak of his *Golden Bough* phase. "It wasn't that important, I guess. Just a ... just a holiday." He had travelled in hopes of witnessing the *Compare e Comare* di San Giovanni. Frazer had written about a rite that was practised in villages in Sardinia every year at the summer solstice. He saw it as a celebration of Adonis. Peter was a different person then, he told himself. Still searching. Still collecting other people's beliefs. Still on the outside, not willing to wade right into anything. Not ready for total immersion as he was now.

"This is the really hard part," whispers Deacon Paul.

Peter realizes he has stopped walking. The water laps about his thighs just above the knees. Deacon Paul must be beginning to imagine he has lost his calling, his commitment, so he lunges forward to prove him wrong; and then it hits him, what Paul meant.

He is looking straight at Julie when the icy water grabs his balls. His whole body convulses; he fears he might even faint. Embrace the danger, the discomfort, the inconvenience, he tells himself. Julie appears blurry from behind his tears, a kind of soft-focus head-and-shoulders water nymph on her lily pad.

In Ozieri, Frazer reported, a young man and a young woman stood on either side of a bonfire, each clutching one end of a long stick that they pass three times rapidly through the flames. The threefold thrusting of their hands into the fire sealed their relationship.

"Are you all right? It really hits you, doesn't it? Right there."

"Fine. I'm fine."

A broken-off piece of an unidentifiable aquatic plant drifts by. Peter thinks about Frazer's Sardinian maidens fashioning their pots out of cork, filling them with the dark earth, sowing a handful of barley. This happens every year late in May — not long after Peter arrived in Ozieri. The sea was still cool, but he had swum every day anyway in Persephone's tears.

"Do you want to rest a minute? Catch your breath?"

They water the pots and keep them in the sun. By St. John's Eve the corn has sprouted and has a good head on it.

Peter squeezes the tears from his eyes to bring Julie into focus. He lowers his gaze to try to see her legs beneath the water, to root himself, remind himself, but the suspended mud and the floating robe interfere.

Then each girl, accompanied by her sweetheart, carries the pot with the stalks of grain through the village to the church. A little procession forms behind them. They smash the pot by throwing it against the church door, and then they all sit in the grass and eat eggs and herbs. Later comes the bonfire.

He lied to Julie when she asked about the scarring on his hands. "A little mix-up with firecrackers," he said. "Twenty-fourth of May, years ago." He had allowed her to kiss the puckered skin, confident she would not be able to smell the Sardinian bonfire on it.

She smiles at him now. It is the performance smile,

the evangelical smile. He tries to distinguish it from the one she gives him when they are alone, but cannot. Deacon Paul takes a step back.

"What is your name?"

And all he can think to say is "N or M." But he knows that's not the right answer this time.

His forehead is running with sweat, although his feet and balls are frozen.

He tastes the rust of blood. Then eggs and herbs. He hears the dull thud of a cork pot broken on a church door.

Total immersion. In fresh water. It was what he thought he had wanted. What he has committed to. If only the lake weren't so cold. If only Julie weren't so bewitchingly beautiful. If only he was really sure that there really was only one way.

As he brushes past Deacon Paul, he can hear Julie desperately pressing on. "Have you repented towards God? Peter?" She calls after him again: "Have you ..." But the rest is drowned out by the purposeful slosh-slosh of his thighs, and then his shins, and finally his wounded feet, as they part the muddy waters and make for shore.

He thinks of the enormous bonfire he will kindle to dry himself off. Tomorrow he will drive to the strait and bathe in the sea and let the salt dry stinging on his flesh.

Jesus

Jesus plays in the quartet at the *kurmittelhaus* three days a week. It's good money — better than he could get back home, not that he would ever go back. There's a lot of Mozart. The spas here all promise a lot of Mozart. Jesus doesn't like Mozart much, but he's glad that at least he's not working at Bad Ischl where they have to play a steady diet of Lehár. One day, he hopes to be able to take a seat in the local *philharmonisches orchester*. They have released a CD and play in all the better halls. But, until the day when one of the violists drops dead and makes room for him, he has decided he will be contented with the *kurorchester*, and the way things are with his life.

The same advertising materials that guarantee Mozart also feature coloured photographs of radiantly naked young women pink in saunas and taut on massage tables. Jesus has never actually seen, anywhere on the streets of Bad Reichenhall, even one woman who remotely resembles those pictured in the photos. This led him, when he first arrived, to believe that they all stayed inside, sweating and being pummelled; but now he thinks that maybe they are altogether imaginary. That they exist on the glossy brochures alone. And in people's minds. Under the mattress in his room at Frau Neumann's, he keeps copies of three of the nicest flyers, plus a page of massage-therapy photos that he downloaded from the internet one day in a coffee shop. In his student days — he likes the sound of that for the four years of subsidized torture just barely past — there were plenty of girls at the Mozarteum like the ones in the ads, only not naked. He would imagine them, though, without their clothes — kneeling behind the doors of practice rooms, heart-shaped bottoms resting on pink-soled feet, sucking on their reeds to moisten them; or with violins tight-wedged under determined chins, the crook of the neck and the arc of the bow arm plotting a new curve for the right breast; or with the rubbed wood of their gleaming cellos clenched between pale dimpled trembling knees. Meanwhile, he carried on a relationship, for a period of not quite two months in his third year, with a girl who let him see as much as he wanted of her actual breasts, her belly, her thighs, her bush, and even, once, because she thought he might like it, her asshole. She was on the cleaning staff in the residence, her skin the colour of his, her eyes, her hair, all like looking in the mirror, like going home. When he made love to her, though, he kept his eyes tight shut, closed his ears to her little moans of pleasure uttered in a language he was ashamed he only barely knew, and imagined instead she was the buttery German girls, the Austrians, the music students who seldom spoke to him. Eventually, she figured this out and stopped coming to see him.

He enters the *kurgarten* at the far end of the thornbush walk. It's the way he always comes to work. He stops to read the plaque, though he knows it by heart, which explains how the wall along the walk is made up of thousands of bushes of *weissund schwarzdorn*. He is awed, as he knows he is supposed to be, by the figure of exactly how many cubic metres of brine are trickled down them each day to create the healthful inhalation effect. The wall of thorn bushes is easily ten metres high and seventy-five metres long. It's not the same one that was there when the site was a gradation house for the old salt evaporation operation, but Jesus has been told that that is how the therapy originated. When they closed down *die alte saline*, and stopped producing their salt that way, someone noticed that if you walked on the leeward side of the thorn bush wall you got a saturated salt breeze, good as going to the seaside. Jesus knows a boy who works at the *salzmuseum*, who is full of information on the history of the place. Sometimes he lets this boy practise his English tour on him. Jesus never offers any correction, even though there are some fairly significant torturings of the idiom in the boy's speech.

Because he is standing at the very end of the walk, he can see that there is a pair of old people beginning to hobble down the windward side of the bushes. He calls after them: "*Entschuldigen Sie, bitte!*" They turn, look at him warily as though he might be expected to rob them. "*Dieser seite ist besser.*" He accompanies the fractured German with what he means to be universal gestures first of direction and then of well-being, finally breathing deeply and nodding furiously as he points to the other side of the wall. The old couple shake their heads and continue down the wrong side of the walk. Jesus laughs and sets off along the leeward side, making a point of taking breaths deep enough for all three of them. He is reminded of the seashore at home, and of how the German word for lake is *see*, which looks like it should sound like sea, but doesn't, and has nothing to do with seeing either, which he supposes makes a kind of sense since you can't see any sea here. Only smell it.

Inside the lobby of the *kurmittelhaus*, the woman behind the desk nods at Jesus. It is neither a friendly gesture nor a hostile, merely a simple acknowledgement that he exists and might reasonably be expected to come through the door at about this time three days a week. He stops as he always does at the plastic-cup dispenser, inserts a coin (they are still so shiny, so newly minted), and pulls on the end of the stack until a cup is released. He knows about the bank of switches behind the desk, and how the woman will turn off the flow to the fountain if you bring your own drinking vessel. When he was still new here he watched her one day trying to train a young backpacking couple as they attempted to fill their large plastic bottles. As they approached each spout in turn, the water would stop. Then the first one started up again — until they returned to it. A woman in a dirndl came in, bought a cup, held it under a spout and the water flowed. When she passed out into the *kurgarten*, the couple tried to take her place, but the water stopped again. Finally, Jesus intervened, having divined what was going on. "I think you're supposed to pay for a cup, if you want the water," he said. They were Americans, maybe Canadians, he couldn't tell, but he knew they would understand English.

"Fuckin' rip-off," the young man had said, but the young woman had smiled and thanked him, fumbled in her jeans for a coin. Jesus had left them drinking cup after cup of the salty water.

He starts with the warm water always, pausing to look up at the cherub perched on top of the fountain, as if to ask permission. From certain angles, it looks as if the cherub is holding himself in his right hand. Jesus always smiles at this as he swishes the warm water around in his mouth. Swallowing is the hard thing. The first few times he had to fight hard to subdue the spit reflex; the water tasted so much like a rinse he used to use for canker sores. Now, he manages to swallow it down without visible flinching. He always moves clockwise around the fountain to the nearest cold spigot. If there is someone in the way, he waits. Some rituals are worth preserving. He knows he should limit himself to three glasses of the cold, or else he'll have to pee during the *konzert*, but today he allows himself four. This is the water from the Karl Theodor spring, the boy from the museum has told him. Once treasured as the primary brine in the salt-making, it is now so diluted by *wild wasser* as to be useful only for drinking in the spa. Still, the pump that has been pulling water from the spring for over two hundred years keeps going, powered by a bottom-action water wheel that is 103 metres away and connected to the pump by an elaborate rod-linkage system. Jesus likes to think, as he drinks his water, about all the labour, all the ingenuity, that has gone into bringing it to him.

The plastic cup lands on the top of the pile of cups in the garbage container. No cup ever seems to nest in another. Jesus thinks about the odds of that for a moment before leaving the lobby. He always thinks about the odds, though he never comes to a conclusion about their significance.

The therapy rooms that line the corridor between the lobby and the *konzert* room are still a mystery to Jesus. At first, he wanted desperately to push on the doors, to peek inside to see what was going on. That was when he still clung to some shred of belief in the advertisements, and half expected to find the naked girls of his fantasies glowing like fleshy light bulbs under the galvanic ministrations of white-coated doctors. But back then he was too timid, too afraid that, looking on all that beauty, he might be cast from paradise, fired from the quartet that called itself an orchestra. Now that he feels secure in his job, he no longer has the desire to look. He has seen too many of the pathetic specimens that come here on the national health bill, has heard too much of psoriasis and ichthyosis (which is either fish-skin or extreme egotism) to want to look. The waters of the Gruttenstein spring are used in these therapy rooms. (Do they drink them or bathe in them, he allows himself just enough curiosity to wonder.) Strong brine, nearly twenty-six per cent, he has been told. They also do work with neurological patients behind these doors, he has heard. Salt has apparently something to do with nerve impulses and muscle contractions and not just high blood pressure. In the thirteenth century, Castle Gruttenstein was built above Bad Reichenhall to defend the salt springs. The mere thought of the treatments going on behind the therapy-room doors is enough to defend them from Jesus.

He is the last to arrive at the *konzert* room. It is always that way. The three women with whom he plays are always there waiting when he arrives. He supposes their arrivals are all synchronized, just as they all play together in perfect instinctive time, though he has no way of knowing. It has become important to him to be the last, just as it is important to him not to see any of the women outside of the *konzert* room. It's not that they don't get along, couldn't be friends, but he likes to keep the chambers of his life separate from one another. When the women suggest that they work up some new repertoire, which would, of course, involve practice outside of strict working hours, he always comes up with a reason why he can't just then. So they stick to a medley of Mozart and Fritz Kreisler that seems to work with the patients; and Jesus keeps his lives discrete and in order.

Halfway through *Eine Kleine Nachtmusik*, Jesus regrets the fourth glass of cold water. Fool, he chastises himself. You were thirsty, he answers back, it will be all right. He realizes that his bow has not moved for three bars, and races his mind rapidly through the distant memory of the score to catch up. The cellist glares at him. He wonders how she would like it if she had to pee, but thinks it's unfair to compare: her legs are wide open. He crosses his, which causes him to miss another couple of bars. When he's on track again, he sneaks a peek out at the faces in the audience. They are all smiling vaguely, a few nodding in time to the music; nobody has noticed his lapses. The cellist can fuck off. Maybe he will tell her so one day.

They are called back for an encore. They are always called back for an encore. Jesus thinks it has something to do with the patients' notion that they might somehow be stretching the government's money more responsibly by getting an extra five minutes of music, or maybe they think their cure will be that much quicker if they prolong the *kurkonzert*: like drinking an extra glass of the waters each day, or spending an extra fifteen minutes inhaling the breeze through the thorn bushes. Jesus very nearly wets his pants on the final bow.

His fellow players invite him for a drink. They always ask. He always thanks them and says no. They remind him of the young women of the Mozarteum who seldom spoke to him, and somewhere deep down he supposes he thinks he is punishing them for that. He tells himself that he makes up for it by never imagining these three women naked with their instruments. By the time he comes out of the bathroom, they have packed up and left.

When he is halfway down the corridor, a door opens, and he can actually see for the first time ever into one of the therapy rooms. Before he can avert his gaze, he registers a crone whom he judges to be at least ninety, seated in a large tub. The surface of the water, a brine so concentrated it is turning red, stands half way up her abdomen, cutting off the lower curves of the brown-spotted breasts that float lazily in front of her, their dark nipples, like hippo eyes, staring accusingly at Jesus. Perhaps she will come out looking like one of the women in the advertisements, he thinks. Then: perhaps she went in looking like one. An attendant appears and shuts the door, and Jesus hurries down the hall, thinking about Parma ham.

He stops for another round at the fountain, even though he knows that Kurt and the others will probably already be waiting for him. The delay is important, another part of the ritual. He smiles at the woman behind the desk. She looks back impassive. He smiles up at the cherub, who still appears to be holding himself. The second plastic cup, the one he buys after the *konzert*, he always leaves on the pink marble lip of the basin, as if he might be back at any minute to reclaim it. He doesn't ever come back, though, not until the next day that he has to play.

Twilight has fallen when he leaves the lobby. He thinks what an inappropriate image that is, like it's a curtain, something final and decisive that actually drops. He stands for a moment on the steps, listening to the water trickling over the thorn bushes, tasting the faint salt of the fountain in his mouth. They don't know the exact source of any of this water, that's what the boy he knows from the museum has said, that they don't know exactly where it comes from in the mountains or when it will dry up or change its course, leaving the ancient pumps in the *alte saline* to wheeze away in vain.

Kurt and the others are sitting on the grass in a clump of bushes on the windward side of the thorn wall. They are drinking bottles of Zipfer, which they bring in from Austria, so easy now there are no real borders. Jesus knows Klaus-Dieter and Georg. They work with Kurt at the *Neue Saline*, not in the part that produces the salts for industrial uses but in the part that produces the eating salt. Most of the young men of Bad Reichenhall who don't work at the cure houses work in the saline. Kurt, who has a little English from the Gymnasium and a finely tuned ear for irony, makes a play on the town's name whenever he is with Jesus. "Reichenhall means very rich in the salt," he says, "How can that be Bad?" Georg has a goiter, and Klaus-Dieter has terrible teeth. Jesus supposes that the iodization and fluoridation came too late for them.

Tonight there is a stranger with them. Also a salt worker, Jesus can tell from the ring he wears: the crossed pick and hammer of the *salzbruderschaft*. He is not drinking Zipfer but Schonram. Kurt explains that this man, whose name is Günter, works in the *salzbergwerk* at Berchtesgaden. Jesus knows that most of the Reichenhaller salt is now made from brine that is piped in from the mine at Berchtesgaden almost twenty kilometres away. He has had it explained to him how the miners there drill down into the hazelnut rock, fill the shaft with water till a funnel shape is eaten away. It's called *sinkwerk*. When the rock has dissolved to form the right-shaped chamber, they keep it filled to the ceiling, sucking out debris from the bottom and pumping out the concentrated brine that sits on the top. A kind of artificial, and much more efficient and reliable, brine spring. He tries to show Günter that he understands his work. "*Sinkwerk*," he says, nodding, as he takes a sip of beer from a bottle that Kurt passes him.

"*Ne*," says Günter, sounding part horse, Jesus thinks. It is as though he is mortally offended at the very mention of the word *sinkwerk*.

"What's wrong?" Jesus asks Kurt, as Günter launches into what is obviously a diatribe, though he speaks so quickly and his accent is so thickly Bavarian that Jesus cannot understand him.

"He does not like to be confused with the brine part in the operation. He says he is the real miner, not the water miner. He hammers the rock."

"By hand?"

"My god, no. There is big machine. He drives the big machine. Very powerful machine. Smashes through anything." Kurt speaks in hushed tones to show his respect.

The darkness comes on quickly now. The last murmurs of guests in the *kurgarten* have subsided. The men drink their beer in silence for a while. Jesus knows what is next. First Georg stands up and mutters something about having a pee. He disappears into the lengthening shadows. Jesus counts to sixty in his head and pleads the same need.

Georg is waiting for him under a myrtle, his fly already unzipped. He keeps his eyes closed as soon as he has made sure that it is Jesus who has stretched out beside him. His hands are already clutching the grass. Jesus knows that soon they will be pulling it out in clumps. He reaches inside Georg's pants, efficient as a therapist. It never takes long, though Georg always encourages him to keep pumping after it is over. He watches Georg's face, the eyelids fluttering, the mouth coming open, the goiter bobbing up and down. This is pleasure, Jesus thinks, not unhappy that he can give it. Georg says nothing as he cleans up and zips up. There is no language between them but what they have already said. Georg vanishes and is almost instantly replaced by Klaus-Dieter, for whom the cure is identical. Jesus wonders sometimes whether they compare notes. The only difference is that Klaus-Dieter always emits a cloud of halitosis at the moment of crisis. Jesus supposes it has something to do with his rotten teeth.

Kurt is another matter. Jesus ministers to the other two out of fear, because it seems a small price to pay for their protection in the town. A man who looks a little different cannot be too careful in a strange country, no matter how little a difference. Kurt he lies with, he thinks, out of a kind of love. At first it was fear, like the others, but now it is mixed with at least a little love, Jesus is sure. Kurt, he believes, keeps his eyes open the whole time, unashamed. At least he knows that Kurt's eyes are open before he guides Jesus's head down, and they're open when it's all over. He tastes like salt, Jesus is always surprised to find. And every time is a little different, as though Kurt doesn't quite know the actual source and has to discover it new over and over again. Being with Kurt excites Jesus. With the others, it is a therapy he delivers. With Kurt, it is a cure as much for himself.

Jesus waits a full two minutes before following Kurt back to the beer-drinking bushes. He listens to the water dripping off the thorn bushes and tastes Kurt, but he does not touch himself. Then he crawls out from under the myrtle.

He finds Günter alone. The others have gone, taken their empty bottles with them. Günter smiles. Jesus smiles. He says the others' names, with a question mark after them. "Vamoose," Günter says and laughs. Jesus is not sure whether this is an attempt to make contact across some cultural gulf. He looks at his watch, expresses alarm, and begins to say goodnight. Günter is up and right beside him before he has the last word out.

Jesus does not like to be kissed, not by anyone, and Günter stinks of sweat and Schonram. He tries to run away, but misjudges in the growing dark and stubs his toes against the trough that runs along the base of the thorn bush wall, to catch the water as it falls. Günter, behind him, lifts him like a sack over the low rim of the trough. The water is cold and bites his feet and ankles. The bushes are sharp and scratch his face. The salt of his tears, mixed with the brine falling from above, stings the cuts. He is grateful, though; these lesser pains give him a place to put his mind while the miner goes to work.

Blood pressure rises, synapses fire off, muscles contract, release, contract. Here, his face pressed into the windward side of the thorn-bush wall, Jesus moves his lips enough to make a vow to St. Rupert that tomorrow he will leave Bad Reichenhall, and give up salt completely. He is fairly sure it's a vow he will keep. As long as he doesn't look back.

Rupert and Sophia

One

Whenever she can get away from the mice, Sophia checks her laptop. You have to stay on top of these things. The bidding can get fierce. Sherry, who works in the lab with her two days a week, makes a joke every time she hears the clicking of the keyboard. She'll call out: What are you doing in there, Sophia? Is it porn? Anybody I know? At first Sophia used to say she was checking her stocks, the weather forecast, or entering data, even though she always left her clipboard on the counter by the cages. Now she doesn't respond. Fortunately, Sherry is not curious enough to follow her into her cubicle to look at her screen. Maybe she is afraid it really is porn. More likely, she is just worried about losing her job. Sophia doesn't consciously try to intimidate the graduate students, but they are scared of her anyway, and she has never taken steps to change that.

It makes them work harder, she thinks, which is what Dr. Morton would want. It also underlines who is permanent and who is not, in case any of them should get any ideas. Once, when one asked her how she had got her job as lab supervisor, she lied, said she had been recruited from another lab when in fact she had herself been one of Sal Morton's graduate assistants. No point in giving them any ideas. Dr. Morton and she are an excellent team. She loves her work, even though she seems to spend more and more of her working hours on the auction sites.

Leaving Sherry to change the water bottles on the cages, she slips around the divider and into her chair. "Did you hear the rumour that they're monitoring all our machines?" Sherry calls after her. "Or is it only the grad students'? Anyway, you might want to be careful in there. Big Brother and all that. Ha ha." The laugh makes Sophia wish she actually were about to check out some porn, since Sherry so obviously thinks she never would. She strokes the mouse pad and her screen saver disappears. There are only twenty minutes left in the auction. It's a good thing she is vigilant. Saltydawg2 has the high bid now. Whoever he is, he shows up at the worst times, often beating her out for something she has her heart set on. She is sure it must be a man. Typing furiously, she sends a new bid by Salaria32, then returns to help Sherry measure the un-drunk water in the bottles she has unclipped.

While Sherry reads off numbers and records them

on a chart, Sophia lets her mind drift back to the auction. She tries to imagine Saltydawg2's reaction when Salaria32 overtakes him, but without a face to picture that isn't much fun. When he was relatively new on the auction scene, she had tried to imagine what he looked like. Once, coming across an engraving in a book about Austria, she decided to give the obviously imperialistic Saltydawg2 the face of an archbishop who, she read, tried to corner the market in salt in baroque times. Wolf-Dietrich von Raitenau, his name was. She liked that he could be both wolf and rat. But the problem with an engraving is the linearity. It's hard to animate expressions other than the single one captured by the artist's lines. So now she doesn't bother to picture Saltydawg2 but focuses on what she feels sure he is about to lose. This time, it is a fairly whimsical item, not at all his usual line. A pink depression hen-on-nest saltcellar is certainly not an aesthetic object, and really only valuable if you have a series of other hens on other nests. Hers are in depression green, and bloom lilac, amethyst, and even Vaseline opalescent. She has bid against him before for the more mainstream hexagonals and oval saw-tootheds, and once for a cobalt blue boat-shaped, but never a kitten and never a hen. She has assumed that he views those as beneath him. He is much more active in the silver line. Although she does not bid on much of that herself, she sometimes checks the bidding histories just for fun. His username shows up regularly in auctions that cover the full range, from trencher to cauldron to capstan to boat. He also seems particularly fond of the seashell spoons. One time he got an exquisite specimen with a rising Venus on its handle. Sophia wished she had bid on that one herself.

"The minuses are definitely going for the saline solution," says Sherry, "just like always. At least the unaltered minuses are. The doc should be happy about that."

Sophia thinks about Sal Morton: how every afternoon when she presents him with the day's results he smiles as though she has just made his night. The findings have been consistent for months, but still he greets each new installment as if it's at once a revelation and a reassurance. He has always been like this, ever since she first worked as his graduate assistant. Sal Morton was one of those people who made you feel valued, important, loved. Not that there was anything sexual between them, or had ever been the suggestion of anything like that, whatever some of the more cynical graduate students might have thought. He made you feel comfortable just by being around. They were easy, at ease, in one another's company.

"The old doc's got quite a lot to be happy about right now, I guess."

Sophia hesitates. She doesn't want to let on that Sherry might know more than she does. "You've heard some rumour about the grants?"

"I was thinking about his personal news."

Sophia is about to remind Sherry that Dr. Morton's personal life is none of their business. The truth is, she has always thought of their life together in the lab as *being* his personal life. It is hers.

But Sherry pushes on: "The engagement and everything."

Sophia drops her pen on the floor. She is afraid she might throw up as she leans to retrieve it. "Oh yes, the … the engagement." When has he had time to meet someone? Why has he needed to?

"They say she's really smart, like some kind of child prodigy or something. Not that she's a child, but she's younger than Dr. M. Are you okay?"

"We should do the readings for the altered group now."

They move on to the cages that hold the ovariectomized mice.

Two

Rupert is not at all dismayed when Salaria32 registers a new bid on the ghastly depression-glass saltcellar. He couldn't care less about winning the auction. A hen on a nest is hardly something he would be able to display, and he would never sell it on to anyone. He has a reputation to uphold, and it is built on zero-tolerance for kitsch, no matter how age may have inflated its market value. The bidding was a way to pass the time. Since Annie announced she was going on vacation without him and then packed her bags and did, he has found the hours hanging heavy. It is not that he and his sister talk all that much. They hardly run into one another in the large house. But since she has been gone he feels her absence keenly. He blames her going away for his sudden lapse in judgment in bidding on the hen. Thank God that Salaria32 has stepped in and saved him from himself. He logs off and heads for the kitchen.

Normally, he would be at work by now, but his asthma is misbehaving. Anyone happening by the shop will have to work out that the hands on the clock on the cardboard sign in the window actually refer to ten o'clock *tomorrow* morning. Business is never brisk on a Monday anyway, and if he misses a sale or two he will still be able to pay all his bills. That is never a concern, which is why he is able to take joy from the shopkeeping — that's what he tells Annie when she wonders why in hell he doesn't give it up and try something else.

He has forgotten to shop, but there is an egg, which he boils, and he finds two pieces of frost-furred bread in the freezer. These he toasts and stands in the silver rack he has brought home from the shop. Then he puts the lot — the egg in its pewter cup, the toast rack, jam pot, knife, spoon, pepper, a chipped Wedgewood plate he has used since he was a child — onto a cedar tray and carries it into the dining room. Eleven o'clock. Brunch then. He does not open the curtains, preferring the luster that the electric light gives to everything around him.

Most of the furniture belonged to his parents and their parents: a mahogany table bought in Edinburgh on

a wedding trip before the first war, matched by a sideboard bought fifty years later at a Ward-Price auction
in Toronto; silver coffee urns and trays that whisper, in
filigreed letters, of service to this or that worthy cause;
and, on the raspberry walls, rows and rows of Bartlett's
Prints of the Canadas. To house his special collection
of cellars, there is a corner cabinet made for him by a
friend, its narrowly spaced mahogany shelves fitted with
tiny lights to show each specimen to best advantage.
Once, some friend of Annie's, invited for dinner in one
of his sister's misguided matchmaking attempts, asked
him why he did not have at least one of them on the
table. She laughed when he told her they were to look at,
that he had never filled even one of them with salt. He
asked Annie not to invite the friend back, which Annie
said was what the friend had asked for too.

The paper this morning features a tiny article that
most people would miss. It's about the recovery of
Cellini's famous *saliera*, the one he made for François I.
After three years, the thieves have finally led the Austrian
police to its hiding place. There is no photograph of
the piece, but Rupert can see it quite clearly in his mind's
eye. Neptune sits across from a lithe young woman
generally supposed to represent the earth. He is holding
his trident at roughly the angle of a moderate erection;
the nymph appears to be pinching her left nipple. At
least that's the way it looks in the official images that
are circulated by the Kunsthistorisches Museum. Rupert
has not been to Vienna. To Neptune's right, the young

woman's left, is the bowl for the salt, and on the other side, beneath the young woman's thigh, is a small temple that doubles as a drawer for pepper. Now that it has been recovered, Rupert thinks he might like to make a trip to see it. If Annie can go off at the drop of a hat, so can he. If only travelling didn't make his stomach ache. He clips the article out, using the candle-trimming scissors that sit on the sideboard; and then he goes upstairs to shave and dress.

Three

Sophia leaves work at exactly five o'clock on Monday. Leaving on the dot is something she has never done, but the news of Dr. Morton's engagement, confirmed to Sherry by the man himself when he paid his daily visit at three, has shaken her. She needs to go home. Winning the auction for the pink depression hen has done nothing to console her. What will she do with another empty saltcellar anyway? Her shelves are full, and, besides, she doesn't really even like the kitsch ones. She bids on them because she can be sure of winning them. Usually. Until Saltydawg2 invaded her turf.

On the bus, she tries to figure out how Sal Morton can possibly have met a woman and become engaged. She knows his rhythms, his gestures. She should have been able to read a change, even if he let nothing slip. So intent is she on replaying the past few weeks searching for clues, she misses her stop and goes two beyond. When she does get off, at the bottom of King Street, she decides to walk across Prince William before tackling the hill by way of Princess or Duke. The shops are closed, which is how she likes them best. Pausing at each window to look in, she is surprised each time at the pale reflection of a gaunt thirty-something woman that gazes back at her before disappearing. She is about to cross the street when she remembers the antique store. Although she has never been in, she likes what the owner does with the windows. So she walks along a little farther, peers through the glass. And has one of those heart-stopping moments she always imagined sex must be like.

Most people would miss it among the array of chased goblets and picture frames and watch fobs, but it is the first thing Sophia spies. It is almost certainly Georgian, cauldron-shaped with a cobalt liner and gadroon border. It stands on three gracefully curved legs that end in tiny hoofed feet. Perfectly plain except for the border. About 1745, she thinks; not later than 1760. Her breath begins to steam up the window. She uses her sleeve to wipe it off, but doesn't stop looking. She is only vaguely aware of people passing by her on the sidewalk. Most give her a wide berth as if she is a street person having an episode, a thief planning a heist. Time ceases to be. She couldn't tell afterwards whether she stood fifty seconds or fifty minutes in front of the window. Finally, someone brushes against her, mutters an apology and hurries on. She looks at the cardboard clock in the shop window, its hands set to ten o'clock, and then, just in case, she depresses the brass thumb lever on the door. It moves, but the door will not be pushed. Bolted. A hexagonal sticker describes how the premises are protected by alarm. Then she continues along Prince William, crosses at Princess, and begins to climb the hill.

Four

Tuesday is one of those rainy days that make Rupert wish he had used his parents' insurance money to move away from the city, or that he had not saddled himself with a shop to open. If he had not stayed home all day Monday, he might have simply punched the alarm clock, rolled over, and waited till the pinging against his windows stopped. But he knew he had some kind of vague responsibility, since he had made the decision to have a shop, to make it available to customers, however unlikely it was that anyone would venture out in this rain just to browse for antiques. Once he has opened up, though, he is glad he braved the storm. He decides the shop is cozier than home right now. With the DSL, he is able to keep up on his auctions all day if he wants to, and the fridge is better endowed than the one at the house. None of the stock he has for sale is as nice as the things he has at home, but it is all nearly as familiar, without any of the sadness of permanence.

He was pleased to see that Salaria32 got the pink

depression hen, but when he notices that she is now bidding on a nice-looking cobalt hexagonal he decides to register a bid several dollars above what he believes it to be worth, just to keep her in her place. Before he hits the submit button, he reassures himself the bid is not purely spiteful; he actually does like cobalt glass cellars. And value, he knows better than many, is whatever someone is willing to pay. It appeals to his sense of irony that, even when developments in science and technology made salt itself a relatively worthless commodity, that had absolutely no effect on the perceived value of the vessels for it. When Cellini made the gorgeous *saliera* for François I, it probably seemed a perfectly fitting way of presenting an extremely precious substance. Now, the piece, valued at $55-million at the time it was stolen, might hold a few cents' worth of salt.

Rupert is in his tiny office behind the cash, eating a toasted bagel with peanut butter, when the chime sounds to tell him someone has come into the shop. He checks his watch: 12:15; not the longest he has had to wait for a customer, but near it. They would come along just as he is having his lunch. Some days, he locks the door and turns the cardboard clock's hands to one o'clock, but today with the rain he thought he was safe enough. He decides to leave whoever it is to do a little browsing while he finishes his bagel — it's nicest while it's still hot — but then he hears her voice.

"Hello? Are you open? Hello?"

What does she think? That he leaves the door unlocked when he's shut? "I'll be right with you," he calls, his mouth sticky with peanut butter.

Sophia is surprised when Rupert emerges from the office. From his voice, she has not expected him to be so tall, or so carefully dressed. "I'm sorry. You were probably on the phone or something. I've interrupted you."

Rupert wants to offer her a towel; her hair is dripping. He is concerned for her health almost as much as he is worried about the finish on the vanity she is standing beside. But he knows that strangers don't offer one another towels, so he says instead: "Is there something particular you were looking for?" He supposes she will be the type that asks to see highboys and then maybe leaves with some linens or a brooch.

"This." She has marched directly to the window, leaned in and lifted out the Georgian saltcellar. Then, embarrassed by her boldness, she replaces it. "That saltcellar."

"I have no spoon for it, I'm afraid."

"What?"

"There is no spoon. It's something of an orphan. Not very useful without the spoon. Unless you're a pincher." He regrets it the moment it leaves his lips.

She smiles. "No, not a pincher. I have plenty of spoons."

"You do?" Rupert looks her up and down again. He guesses she is in her early thirties, with a neat figure, as far as he can tell beneath the raincoat, and a face that reminds him of someone, though he is sure they have never met.

"Seventeen-forties?" she asks, and then worries he might think she's a show-off. It's just that she doesn't want him to think she's going to be someone who is easy to fool. She is an aficionado. She has earned her right to that status, and will not be taken advantage of.

"Forty-five, as near as I have been able to determine."

"The liner is original?"

"Oh yes. Would you like to hold it again?"

When he hands it to her his hands shake a little. Hers do too.

"Should I have a glove?" she asks.

"I have all day to polish things. Not that your hands are —"

"It is beautiful. The feet ..." She stops herself. Too much enthusiasm could inflate his price. She takes a deep breath. "How much ... how much were you thinking?"

"Five hundred."

"Without a spoon? Sorry, I didn't mean to be rude. Five hundred?"

"It is a fine specimen. Beautiful, as you say."

She hands it back to him, trying to keep her body language ambiguous. She wants him to wonder for just an instant whether she wants him to wrap it or put it back in the window. "I will have to think," she announces finally.

"Of course." He puts the cellar back, knocking over a picture frame as he does. He thinks about his cold peanut butter. "Is there anything else you'd —?"

"I really should be getting back to work."

"Of course." He is about to wish her a good day.

"Do you think …?"

"Yes?"

"Do you think I could come and have another look, tomorrow maybe?"

"We are open from ten till five. I usually take lunch from —"

"Oh God, I'm sorry. You really aren't open right now are you? It's supposed to be your lunch."

"It's not a problem."

"I'll come later in the day. It's just that I'd like to … I'd really like to bring in one of my spoons, you know, to see how they would get along."

Rupert, who imagines he may be the only person in the world to understand this statement, smiles and says that will be fine.

Five

On Tuesdays, Sophia is alone in the lab. Normally, she uses the quiet to draft reports she thinks might interest Dr. Morton. She might work up a précis of literature she has come across, or rough-in a series of hypotheses that could explain some anomalous results in the experiments. None of this is, strictly, part of her job, and since she is no longer a graduate student there is no real professional need for her to go the extra mile. She does it simply to see the look of gratitude on his face, to hear him say, "Oh Sophia, you shouldn't have. You really are too good."

After her lunchtime visit to the antique store, however, she has trouble concentrating on data or articles or anything but the Georgian cellar, and its seller. She catches herself reversing the positions of the saline and fresh water bottles on one of the cages. When the mail comes in, she sorts hers in with Sal Morton's and has to go back into his office to retrieve it. While she is in there the second time, she notices a new photograph on the corkboard. It shows her boss in a bar with his arm around a very pretty younger woman. Both are wearing name cards, the kind they give you at conferences: hanging in plastic sleeves just above their hearts. So this is the fiancée. Sophia has to fight the urge to poke thumbtack holes through the eyes.

She flees to her laptop and the safe, familiar territory of the auction site. Saltydawg2 has entered another bid for the cobalt blue hexagonal that she really wants. She is about to submit a new number herself when she begins to think again about the Georgian. If she ever hopes to have that, she will have to cut her spending elsewhere. She remembers how casually the man said "five hundred," and how he did not even seem to hint that he might entertain a counter-offer. She thinks about his freckled hands as they held the cellar out to her, trembling a little. He smelled of peanut butter, which some people might not like but Sophia didn't mind. It's obvious he is the owner of the shop. She wonders what would make a person go into that line of work, wonders whether she might have liked it herself. She knows she would have been good at it. And that confidence prompts her to click "submit" and continue her competition with Saltydawg2, whoever he is. Then she begins browsing the net for salt spoons. It's not that she has lied to the man in the shop; she does in fact have several lovely ones, but she is not sure that any of them is quite worthy of the Georgian.

Sophia is sitting on a stool beside the cage that belongs to the unaltered minus mice, looking back and forth between them and the pluses in another cage when Sal Morton comes in for his daily visit.

"Trying to remember which is which?" He loves to make jokes that make you feel you're in a cartoon in *The New Yorker*. If he sees you working with the water bottles on the cages he'll say something like "Absolut Mouse," or "these all-inclusive resorts aren't what they used to be." The graduate students always groan obligingly. Sophia used to find the cracks very amusing. Today, however, she has a hard time managing to force even a faint smile. The fact is, she *has* been wondering about the difference between the two groups. She knows what it is genetically, and she knows why they are working with a group of mice that is oxytocin-blocked and a group that is not, the minuses and the pluses. She even understands why they have also removed the ovaries of half of the members of each group. What she can't imagine is what difference it all makes to the mice themselves, to the way they experience the world. The absence of oxytocin makes them crave salt, that is obvious from the results, but do they notice the absence itself? If they got enough salt, would they realize that what they were actually hungry for was oxytocin?

"Sorry, Dr. Morton. I was a million miles away."

"We all dream sometimes, Sophia. It's okay."

Maybe if she had asked him about his dreams, maybe if they had talked about something other than experimental data and the practical challenges of securing gene-blocked mice, things would not have gone this way. There would be no photo on the corkboard, no speculation among the graduate students over when the boss would set a date. But she had never seen the need.

"I'm in a kind of a hurry today, so I won't have time to look at anything with you, I'm afraid. Maybe you could just put your reports on my desk?"

"There are no reports today."

"Oh. Well, fine. It's time you took it a little easier. We don't want to end up like that cartoon."

She knows the one he means. A giant mouse dressed in a lab coat sits outside a cage where a tiny human is racing madly on a rat wheel. It is a favourite of theirs. Was.

"See you tomorrow, then."

"Yes. Tomorrow."

It's how they have ended every one of his lab visits since she was a graduate student. She always took tremendous comfort from the certainty.

Six

Rupert waits until five-thirty on Wednesday to close the shop, just in case the woman is running late. She seemed quite definite she would be returning to look again at the Georgian cellar. He gave it a special polish after lunch, even though it was nearly perfect as it was and he was quite busy with customers all day. Selling a revolving bookcase, a pair of wine tables, as well as a variety of smaller things that were being duty-bought for birthdays, would normally have counted as a very good day — but, without the woman, it has been something of a disappointment.

Since yesterday he has scarcely had a thought in which she did not figure somehow. Mostly, they have been pure thoughts — wondering what her spoon might look like, whether she empties her cellars after use, if she uses them at all, whether she collects glass as well as silver — although he has also come to identify her more and more with the lithe woman, too skinny to be Demeter, on the Cellini *saliera*. This doesn't count as a sexual fantasy, he decides, because of the mythological content, but it stirs him anyway. It leads him on to other daydreams: of himself as a kneeling boy holding up a shell filled with salt, in the manner of those Victorian pieces he usually abhors; of her as the Venus on that spoon he won on the auction site a few weeks ago.

He moves the short hand of the cardboard clock from one to ten, puts out the lights, sets the alarm, and locks the door. On the way home, he will have to buy something for his supper.

There is a postcard from Annie along with the bills and flyers. Dublin is wonderful, she writes, it reminds her a little of Saint John, only rich now, mostly. She is going on to Salzburg next on Ryan Air, which means she is in Austria now as he reads the card from Ireland. No mention of when she plans to come back. He supposes she has been very careful with her share of the insurance money; she might last several years away.

He checks on an auction he's bidding in. The piece is a spoon that would be perfect with the Georgian cellar in the shop. Interest is high, and Saliera32, who he had pegged as mainly a depression-glass girl, is driving him beyond what it's reasonable to pay. He resents her stubbornness, wishes there were some way to break the anonymity and communicate with her directly his reasons for wanting the spoon. He would tell her how his was a need, while hers could only be a desire. He would not say greed; that would no doubt only provoke her to bid higher. She would listen to reason, he thinks. Anyone would.

He cooks the noodles too long. They are the fresh ones that take so much less time than the dried. The basil in the pesto seems more skunked than sweet, but the wine is crisp and dry. It seems a shame to cork it, since it will never be this good again. He carries the bottle into the den to watch one or two of the thirty episodes of *Seinfeld* that are available every evening. Within twenty minutes he falls asleep. He loses the auction.

Seven

She is waiting outside the shop on Thursday morning when he arrives a little before ten. It is raining again, and she has added rubber boots and an umbrella to the raincoat of the other day. He thinks of the girl on the salt package. What's the slogan?

"Sorry. I know I'm early."

"Not at all. Come in out of the rain. No work today?"

"I'm going in late. I never do that. The mice will cope."

"Mice?"

"Never mind. Should I take my boots off?"

He realizes that his shoes are already in his hands. He keeps a smarter pair just inside the door of the shop. He is about to explain when he realizes she has not waited for his answer. If she was wearing socks, she has managed to slip them off inside the boots. Her nail polish matches exactly the dominant shade in the medallion-cornered *Farahan* on which she now stands, her toes massaging the hand-knotted fibres.

"I ... I waited for you yesterday."

"Oh God, I'm sorry. I ... I had something to do."

"I'm glad you're here now." Jesus. Is that too forward? "I took it out of the window. Because I knew you were interested. I didn't want anyone else ..."

"Thank you. I hoped when I didn't see it there that you had only moved it. I like the new window display, by the way."

"I hadn't changed it for months. That's very bad marketing."

"I suppose."

"You can't leave things as they are for long. I'll get it, shall I?"

Sophia follows Rupert into the little office behind the cash. "Oh. Sorry. Maybe you don't like customers in here."

The tiny room is suddenly full of the smell of her shampoo. "It's okay. The light is not wonderful, though."

"I would know what it looks like in the dark." It is a stupid thing to say, she knows, and can only hurt the negotiation.

"Did you bring the spoon?"

"Not exactly. Maybe we should bring it out onto the counter."

Rupert hands it to her to carry. She takes it like she is receiving a sacrament. When she puts it down Rupert notices that the polish on her fingernails matches her toes. He doesn't remember it from the other day. As they gaze at the cellar their heads are only inches apart. Rupert wishes he had shaved. "What do you think?"

"It's everything I remembered."

"Will it go with your spoon?"

"I think so. I think it will."

"But you didn't bring it? The rain, I suppose."

"No."

"You didn't want to take it on with you to work."

Sophia reaches into her pocket and pulls out a folded sheet of paper.

As she flattens it out, he recognizes immediately the image that is printed on it. It is the same image he revisited on the auction site dozens of times yesterday. Before he fell asleep in front of the television.

"They are shipping it today," she says. "They have these auctions on the internet. Don't you think it will be perfect?"

"I do," says Rupert.

"The thing is," says Sophia, "the thing is I probably can't actually buy the cellar right away. You know, I'd like to see the actual spoon with it." What she really means is that she will have to sell off at least half of her glass collection to raise the money.

"Absolutely. You need to see them together. That's sensible. I'll just keep the cellar in the office for the time being. You could ... you could come and visit it, you know, while you are waiting for the spoon."

"You are very sweet." Before either of them knows it, she has kissed his cheek. Neither of them says anything more as she hurries to slide her bare feet back into her boots. Rupert is already looking forward to tomorrow, when he knows she will come in again.

Salt in the Wounds

1. Mercury

At first, I hope they are coming to fling their bouquets off the back of the ferry. I want it to be something significant — a loving memorial for a drowned friend, a local ritual for appeasing whatever vengeful water god lurks at the bottom of the lake, a sign, an act that might speak of the dark, invisible history of the place. I am owed some acknowledgement, however oblique, that there are more forces here than we can see on this beautiful fall day. But they only want me to take their picture. They lean against the stern rail, flowers tight to breasts, arms about each other's waists. There are three of them: tight leather jackets, big hair, more makeup than I know I should like, but pretty, all of them. Seductive. I suppose you would say they were smiling, though they do not look particularly happy. The one who shows me how to work the camera smells faintly of lilies and has beautifully polished nails. If her two friends weren't along, I would strike up a stumbling conversation. Of course, if her two friends were not along I would not have been asked to take the picture in the first place. The Three Graces of the Chiemsee, I think, as I depress the button. Before I can ask do they want another, the one who smells of lilies has taken the camera from me and all three have hurried back into the cabin, out of the wind.

"A wedding, do you think?" I hear a man ask his pregnant wife. They are Americans who became as frustrated as I did trying to communicate with the ferry operator when we boarded at Prien. Like most tourists, they amuse themselves by making up stories about the unknowable locals. For them, though, it is only a pastime.

"Not really dressed for a wedding," his wife drawls in response, and I realize she is right. Although only one of the jackets was actually black, the ensembles were uniformly sober: dark pants and shoes, one grey turtleneck and two plain navy scarves. A funeral, then. But why the photo? You don't see many funeral albums. I haven't.

I try to recompose what I saw in the viewfinder, hoping for a clue, something to help me construct the story of these women. I feel I have to know more, but to leave my seat in the late autumn sun to follow them into the shadowy cabin could send the wrong message. You can't be too careful these days. I will have to wait until we all get off the boat. There will be time to observe them on the island, I think. I could always offer to take another picture.

IT'S ANOTHER PHOTOGRAPH, ALSO taken by a stranger, near here but in another time, that has brought me to this place. The image is of a little girl, her limbs scrawny but her face filling out again, a little girl holding a sign with her name written across it. My mother. This was how they tried to reunite families in the first years after the war. The newspapers published photographs of the children in the camps, their tiny hands clutching a card that showed the sum total of what was known of their identity: sometimes a first name, often a nationality; once or twice, wherever it wasn't obvious, the gender. The camp at Kloster Indersdorf was run by the UN Relief and Rehabilitation Administration, which meant, in prac- tice, a number of well-meaning American ladies. After a couple of years of trying to find the parents, these ladies were instrumental in arranging new homes for whatever children were left over. Mother was one of the leftovers. She had left Bremen on the *Aquitania* bound for Halifax in the late summer of 1947. Only decades later, in the very last months of her illness, though, just before the morphine led her mind finally down paths where no one could follow, did I learn any of that. Only when it was obvious that she was safely headed for the end did she become ready to talk about the UNRRA camp near Prien, or about the weeks and months, the other camps, that led her there. My father must have known, of course, but he had guarded her secret to his grave.

After Jan left me and I decided I needed to take a trip, it seemed inevitable that I should use my small legacy to revisit these places on my mother's behalf. I needed to fill in the episodes she had not told and now could never tell. I needed to hear her tale directly from the landscape where it had actually happened.

I avoided Dachau. It would hardly have been much out of my way from the airport at Munich, but it had no part in my mother's story. And neither did I begin with Buchenwald, though that was where her journey actually started. The distance, I told myself, was too great, though it had not proven so for her tiny bleeding feet. The truth was I could not face that chapter directly. I needed to enter the story at the point where it became clear she would survive. So I had begun with Laufen, the town where the SS officer who had escorted her group of fifteen hundred out of Buchenwald made a proposition to the *burgomeister*. He paraded before him the few hundred children who remained alive after weeks of marching; and he told him that if the town did not take the children in he and his men would shoot them all, and then he would see to it that the Americans blamed the towns-people. "Laufen," my mother had mused. "*Laufen* is what they would always be shouting at us. It means 'run.' We could not believe that the town where we were finally freed was called that." She would finish by repeating that it was odd how things turn out, wasn't it? And this would mean she did not want to remember any more.

The Salzach at Laufen runs fast and shimmers a brilliant turquoise-blue, the result of reflection off its polished marble bottom. The current is likely deadly, even though the river looks shallow. A person would not be in over his balls before he was swept away, I think. A beautiful treed path runs for kilometres along the side and you can look across at Austria where an identical trail follows the parallel bank. At intervals, there are large metal signs, writing across the otherwise unspoiled landscape, interrupting the illusion that nothing has changed here for hundreds of years. Each sign bears a number. When you look across, you see the same number on the other side. Whatever it means, I am sure it is very efficient. On my first day, I bicycled from Salzburg, past Freilassing where the Saalach flows into the Salzach. The bicycle trail is marked for tourists with signs bearing a tiny brown silhouette and the words *Mozart Radweg*. It is, I think, unlikely that Mozart travelled these wooded paths. I felt I should be tearing down the markers and replacing them with ones bearing the emaciated silhouettes of children on a forced march. But I have no way of confirming whether they actually passed that way. What few details I have been able to discover do not include an exact route. Every few kilometres all the way to Laufen, I would stop to listen, straining to hear what the land had to tell me, what it might remember of those days: leaves rustled by tiny bruised feet as they marched along, the strains of a child's voice singing to keep its captors from strangling it in its throat. But there was only quiet, and the rushing of the Salzach. Once, I met a man guiding another whose head was completely swathed in bandages; and, a little later, a woman walking her dog. She did not return my mumbled *Grüss Gott*; neither did she warn me that the fork in the path I had chosen would quickly lead to a dead end at a tributary stream where the bridge has long since given up the ghost.

The town of Laufen itself is charming, more Mediterranean than Bavarian somehow. Its steep cobbled streets, its gaily painted houses and ancient church would be hard-pressed to recall a band of starving children and a handful of SS officers. All of that was only a little more than sixty years ago, but this town looks back more than six hundred. It can easily make excuses for its selective memory, I suppose.

The ferry reaches the *herren insel*. The Americans and I pass hurriedly through the cabin to the ramp just aft of the bow where we disembark. Though we do not compare notes, I know they are as terrified as I am of being barked at in German. We do not want to hold things up. *Laufen*, I can hear a ghostly voice shouting. And I do. Only after the boat pulls away from the wharf do I realize that the Three Graces have stayed on, headed, I gather as I consult the posted schedule, for the *frauen insel*. I should have known.

The two islands, the men's and the women's, nearly touch as they fish-hook towards one another. I can imagine the monks swimming across the narrow strait under cover of darkness. The ferry, though, cuts across the open water, covering the greatest distance between the two, perpetuating the cherished illusions of the chaste ninth-century founders of the two communities.

"There is nothing going on here," it seems to want to affirm, like so much I have seen. I watch as the *Berta* shrinks to the size of my fist before I turn away.

I skip the monastery and follow the signs for the *schloss*. When I planned the trip, madly following links on the internet, this place where the new German constitution was born kept coming up. Even if by 1948 my mother was safely settled in Canada, the things that were decided in the palace of mad King Ludwig II seemed like they should be a part of her story — if not a resolution, at least a comment, a footnote.

I take the path marked *Winter*, afraid to be caught in November on the one marked *Summer*. Even though the unseasonably warm weather might provide me with a viable excuse, I do not want to try to argue the point with an official. The path is paved, direct and easygoing, but it delivers me to one side of the palace, and so I miss what must be the intended first impression. Ludwig modelled his *schloss* on the palace at Versailles, and the terraced grounds go on and on in one perfect-bordered rectangle after another down to the Chiemsee. To be delivered by the Summer path out of the surrounding trees and onto one of these terraces, and then to look up the hill and encounter the magnificent building face-on must take your breath away, which is what Ludwig no doubt had in mind: knocking the wind out of his visitors by a trick of the landscape.

I learn too late that tickets for the tour are only sold back near the ferry landing — did I not see the signs?

— so I have to settle for a leisurely circuit of the outside of the building, pausing to look up at intervals to try to detect where the palace is unfinished. Ludwig apparently ran out of money, or interest, or breath; I can't remember which. The place looks fine to me. How much ornament is enough? As I reach the fourth side, I notice on the white stone a tracery of faint lines that I did not see when I first came upon the building. It is the remains of graffiti, or of something more official. It is hard to tell through the veil of years. Despite all of the rubbing that has obviously happened in the interval, the barbed form of a swastika can still be made out. The *hakenkreuz*. Evidence of something, but what? I shudder and head back to the dock.

The *Rupert* approaches from Prien. The schedule says it will return there immediately. I wonder about waiting ten minutes for the other boat, the *Berta,* and trying to upgrade my ticket to permit a trip to the *frauen insel*. I might find the Three Graces. The women's island might hold some sign I should not miss. It is too exhausting, though, just imagining the wrangle with the ferryman that I know would be required to make the change. So I jump on the *Rupert* just as it pulls away, managing to get yelled at anyway. All the way back across the water I look out over the stern towards the women's island, straining to see the Three Graces dancing naked and petal-bestrewn on the beach I know must be on the far side of the island, beyond the spires of the abbey.

In the parking lot at Prien I discover that the side of

my rental car has been scraped. A gash like a mountain stream is cut into the green door, baring the metal beneath. There isn't a car for several spaces on either side, and I look in vain for a note, which I wouldn't have been able to understand anyway. What kind of a person tears the paint off someone's car and drives away? What kind of person sees such things happen and doesn't try to stop the doer? I don't call the police or the rental company. My abilities with the language would not be equal to the challenge. When I return the car in Salzburg, I will simply act surprised and shrug my shoulders to show them that it is all a mystery to me; and then I will pay the deductible if they insist.

TWO DAYS LATER I am sitting in a bus in Bad Reichenhall, trying to tune out the chattering of school children and staring out the window. I see a boy who can't be much more than eleven drag a piece of broken glass across the side of a parked car, leaving a long crooked furrow in the paint job. I watch, and do nothing.

Bad Reichenhall is not part of the official project, not part of the pilgrimage. I have come only because a patient recommended it. As far as I know, my mother and the other children with her were not marched through it on their way to Laufen. Neither does it seem tainted with any of the infamy attached to nearby Berchtesgaden, though I am sure that its thriving salt industry must have made it indispensable to the war effort. It is, my patient has told me, simply a very beautiful little spot, a resort town that might even remind me of places nearer home. He was worried I might become homesick on my travels; that, hemmed in among the Alps, I would begin to yearn for Mahone Bay or the Fundy breezes of St. Andrews by-the-Sea. Besides, he said, the train ride is charming. Because his therapy is at a delicate stage and I do not want to have to report to him that I have not bothered to follow his recommendation, I bought the train ticket, only to discover once we were pulling away from Salzburg, that the line was torn up somewhere around Piding and I would have to transfer to a bus in Freilassing.

I find it hard to see the place through his eyes. The familiarity he promised eludes me. He visited in the summer, of course, at the height of the spa season. Now, in early November, the tourists are mainly gone, and the sun disappears behind the mountains by three in the afternoon. Even the famous thorn-bush walk, where you can inhale the health-giving salt vapours, is shut down for cleaning. I walked its length twice, breathing deeply just in case, but all I got out of it was snippets of a conversation I could not understand between two invisible men who were scrubbing the catch basin.

With no real deadline for my return to Salzburg, but afraid of missing the last bus, I spent much of my time in town circling the train station, reading and rereading, with no more comprehension for each successive effort, the notices that advised how the trains were being replaced by buses for the time being. The word *ersatz* figures prominently in all of the notices, as does *bahnhof-platz*. The buses themselves all wear the single word *ersatz* across their brows, as if it's a badge of honour. They are not otherwise marked that I can see. How to know which one is returning to Freilassing to meet the train for Salzburg and which is going the other way to Berchtesgaden, is not explained. To make matters worse, they all seem to approach the *bahnhof-platz* from the same side — I suppose because of where the access to the highway is. At one point, having observed arrivals and departures with no further insight, and relatively assured that there would be no ersatz train of any description for at least thirty minutes, I ventured along the avenue that I knew my bus must travel on its way to the highway and back to Freilassing. Or on to Berchtesgaden if I made a mistake.

If I had not chosen to cover on foot what I had passed already on the bus and would necessarily pass again on the bus out of town, I would never have seen the shrine.

Not more than a few hundred metres from the *bahnhof*, on the opposite side of the avenue, there is a recreation centre. Beside it, set back from the sidewalk, is a tidy plywood construction, bestrewn with flowers and photographs and flickering votive lights. Laminated newspaper clippings tell the story, as well as I could make it out, of a tragedy not a year old. On the site stood an arena. When I looked up I could see the pillars still there, bare ribs against the backdrop of the mountains. On January 2, 2006, heavy snow had caused the roof to collapse, and fifteen hockey players, all children, had

been killed. Fifteen children in a town this small. It is
hard to imagine the impact. That is why I say nothing
when from my seat on the *ersatz zug* bound for Freilassing I see another boy drag a piece of glass across a car.

In a way that I am almost embarrassed to admit,
the sad little shrine actually gives me hope. It is one
of the few signs that I have seen anywhere here that
the landscape might be allowed to remember terrible
events, however temporarily. Somebody remembers
those children, and they have made a place to do it. For
now, at least.

On the return bus trip to Freilassing, my seatmate
proves to know more English than I know German and
he delights in explaining some of the lore associated
with the various mountains in the area. I listen patiently,
anxious to repay his kindness in helping me finally
identify the correct bus when the drivers insisted on
not understanding my increasingly anxious questions.
The Watzmann, he tells me, is like a father, surrounded
by his *frau* and his *kinder*. His children. It is a little
family. I will see what he means. And then there is *die
Schlafende Hexe*, his own favourite: the Sleeping Witch.
Can I not make out the series of peaks that form her
nose, her chin, and her narrow but surely unmistakable
breasts? Soon they will wear a brassiere of snow. The
interpretations interest me professionally, of course.
They are such obvious indicators of archetypes, especially the pointy-breasted witch. But these are not the
significances I have travelled so far to read out of this

landscape, and I am glad when the man gets off the bus at Hammerau and I am alone with my memories of the little shrine in Bad Reichenhall.

It is not exactly The Sleeping Witch that I have been dreaming of when I awake twelve hours later in my hotel room, my pyjama-bottoms soaked through, sticky. Though the actual dream has already faded, I know that Jan was in it. Before she left me. We were on a trip somewhere. She was always more interested in sex when we were away from home. We must have been some-where south because there were flakes of pink coral sand stuck to her nipples and she tasted of salt. I peel off the bottoms and use the legs to dry myself off. And then I remember Ernest Jones on the subject of Onan's seed It's something he read in Paracelsus, about how mastur-bation produces salt, not real semen at all. And that incubi and succubae are all that can be born of that way-ward ejaculate that does not find its "natural" home. Does a wet dream count the same as jerking off when you're awake? I imagine all of the evil spirits that may be taking life from my crumpled pyjamas as they lie in a heap where I have thrown them. I wonder if Jan ever dreams of me anymore. But I know the answer to that.

ON MONDAY IT LOOKS like rain. I decide to explore Salzburg itself.

I am desperate enough to consider taking a *Sound of Music* tour. I have already been to the Nonnberg Stift. My first day, still jet-lagged but eager for a concert in this most musical of cities, I found an early evening recital in the convent church. It was by a massed choir of school-children watched by proud parents whose cellphones kept going off. Each successive ring tone, which included Mozart and Beethoven as well as some more jazzy riffs, drew glares but apparently did nothing to persuade anyone else to turn off their phone. It was a fascinating blend of indignation and denial. The Aryan soloist, with her thick braid and rosy cheeks, I was interested to see, was carefully balanced by three or four black faces and a couple that could have been Turkish, all arranged so casually in the group as if to say it was ever thus. The adventures of the von Trapp family, I begin to think, may be as close as I am going to get to any acknowledgement whatsoever that the whole area was once overrun by Nazis. "How do you solve a problem like Herr Adolf?" I want to sing. When I look at the brochure, though, it is clear that the tour is only concerned with visiting a few of the more picturesque sites where the movie was shot. The actual story with its sinister backgrounds will not figure much. I decide to save the thirty-five euros that the tour would cost and stroll through the Mirabell Gardens instead.

She is standing beside the statue that the guidebook tells me is Paris carrying off Helen. It is one of four groupings in the middle of the gardens, representing the four elements. This one is intended to stand for water, I read, while Aeneas bearing Anchises is fire, and Hercules battling Antaeus is air. Finally, Proserpina struggling with Pluto is, of course, Earth.

Her fair hair is soaking wet and plastered to her head, although the threatened rain has not actually started yet. Her blue eyes are reflecting pools. "Would you like me to make your photograph?" she asks. I'm not sure how long I have been looking at her. "With Herr Paris and Helena?"

I nod, and then realize I don't have a camera.

"You are not the tourist?"

"I am. A visitor. Von Canada," I try, proud of the effort of that one word.

"But you do not like to make the photograph."

How can I tell her that nothing I want to see, nothing I want to learn about this place, would register through a camera lens? It has all been covered up, it seems. "I lost my camera," I lie. It is easier.

"From Vancouver?" she asks. It's what they all ask.

I explain, no, the other coast, which probably means nothing to her.

She asks if I am liking Salzburg.

"It is very beautiful. Schön."

"It must make you sad to miss your camera then."

"Very sad."

"My name is Andrea."

"Daniel." We shake hands heartily at this point. Her palm is cool and moist.

"Do you like to drink coffee, Mr. Daniel?"

She leads me then out of the garden, past the Landes-theater and along the Schwarzstrasse to the café at the

Hotel Sacher. This and the Tomaselli on the other side of the Salzach, she tells me, are the only real coffee houses left in the city, and far preferable to the newer more chic Demel and its imitators. The waiters barely deign to notice us, which Andrea assures me is a sign that it is a good place. "And do you not find them wonderful silly?" she asks. "All this nose-in-the-air when they are giving us just a coffee?" As it turns out, they have to give us more than just a coffee because she orders a *schnicker* to go with our *verlängerters* — espresso lengthened out with water, she explains, the result being essentially what she calls *Amerikanisch* coffee.

"I like to come here after my swim," she says. "To become warm again." There is an indoor pool just north of the gardens. She tries to go every day.

I tell her she should dry her hair before going outside, she might catch cold; and then I wonder if that is too personal a remark on such short acquaintance.

"And you are the *mediziner* to tell me this advice?" she throws back.

"As a matter of fact, I actually am a doctor."

"And I am the student. Of the medicine. Colds do not happen in this way. There are viruses. We have the new private university now. Paracelsus Medizinische Privatuniversität. You have heard of this?"

I haven't, but I nod in a way that I hope suggests that not only have I heard of it but I might somehow have been responsible for creating it.

"You are a specializer perhaps?"

I admit to being a psychiatrist. She hoots with laughter. Even the snooty waiters look in our direction.

"Excuse me. I remember a joke. That is all."

"Tell me."

"I hope I get it right. How many psychiatrists — is this the correct *aussprache*? The pronouncing? — how many psychiatrists does it need to change a light bulb?"

I shake my head as if I don't know.

"Only the one. But he has to be made sure first that the light bulb wants to change."

I have heard this a thousand times, of course, but she tells it so charmingly that I laugh.

When we leave the café it has begun to rain. I offer my umbrella and she hooks her arm through mine. "Walk with me to the bus?" she says.

Long before we get to the Hanusch-Platz, while we are crossing the Staatsbrucke, she tugs me to the railing of the bridge and holds up her face to be kissed.

Her nose is running a little, but her cool wet mouth tastes like sugar.

2. Sulfur

The cigarette smoke upstairs in the Zirkelwirtshaus is so thick I expect at any moment to stop breathing and drop to the floor. I ask Andrea how people put up with it, especially in a place where food is prepared and eaten. She simply shrugs, says she supposes it is all what you are used to. It's an unusual response from a medical student, I think.

It is Monday night, and the archaeologists have gathered as they do every second week. Andrea tells me she loves to eavesdrop — "to overlisten" is what she actually says — to their conversations. She took a course with some of them once, before she discovered her medical vocation, and she found them to be some of the most fascinating people she has ever encountered.

"They know everything about what is under us," she told me as we dressed in my hotel room. (She did not get on the bus after our kiss.) "I will make a translation for you. You will find it completely fascination."

The restaurant is in the Pfeifergasse, at Papagenoplatz. On the way, trying to show off, I asked Andrea whether the *platz* was named for Mozart's character because of the restaurant, or was it the other way around?

"I do not understand."

"*The Magic Flute* has all kinds of Masonic connections, doesn't it?"

"Does it? I do not like opera. I do not like Mozart." This last she whispers, obviously not firm enough in her convictions to risk being killed for them on the streets of Salzburg. "Why would it matter?"

"Zirkel means compasses, right? It doesn't mean circle."

"It means the thing you use to draw the circle. Or to measure some distance."

"Exactly. And that instrument is also a Masonic symbol. The Zirkel restaurant is somehow connected with

Freemasonry, then, and so is Papageno."

"I think you try too hard to see patterns. Some things are only the *zusammentreffen*."

"Coincidences?"

"You know this word?"

"I guessed."

But I cannot guess at very much of what the archaeologists are saying, so Andrea is kept busy translating. Every now and again she becomes so enrapt in their conversation that she is annoyed when I ask her a question. "Now I have lost it," she will snarl, "and I wanted so much to hear that thing."

Their conversation apparently revolves around excavations that were made two or three years ago, in preparation for the *Viva Mozart!* exhibition just around the corner from where we sit. The archaeologists are still up in arms about how matters were handled. Remains of the foundations of a Roman building, dating from when the city was called Iuvavum, long before Rupert resurrected it and renamed it for the salt he began mining, were uncovered in the courtyard of the Neue Residenz. Then they were simply buried over again. The archeologists would have liked the stones to remain exposed so that visitors could walk among them. The authorities, however, said they thought that could be dangerous, Andrea tells me, so they paved over the site. As a kind of concession, though, they built into the new paving the ghostly outlines of the shapes of the Roman walls below. According to the archeologists, the issue was not one of safety at all. It was simply that the organizers of *Viva Mozart!* did not want their visitors distracted by something so obviously far more interesting than a two-hundred-fifty-year-old composer. Unless you know to look for them, they say, you would never notice the pale lines on the pavement.

"Why do they care so much about Roman ruins?"

"Do you not think it is wonderful to know what is our past?"

"I do think it's important. I just wonder why be so selective."

"I do not know what you are trying to say."

Our food arrives and I am spared an explanation, for the moment.

Andrea quickly loses all interest in the talk of ruins as she dives into the mountain on her plate. The Zirkel is a favourite with students, and obviously the proprietors take an active, nearly parental, interest in seeing that they are well fed. We eat in silence while the archaeologists jabber on and blow out giant clouds of blue smoke. One or another of them seems to be lighting up every minute, and the sulfur smell of matches gets more and more confused with the taste of the *pilz* sauce on my *schnitzel*. When I stop eating, Andrea worries that I do not like it.

"It's just a lot of food for an old guy," I say.

"I will help you." I am hurt that she does not disagree about my age, but relieved when she slides my plate over beside hers — for a moment I was worried she meant to feed me. I order another Zipfer, not because I like it but because I don't know how to ask for anything else.

When Andrea has polished both plates, she tunes in to the archaeologists again. "They are talking of making a map. Of the Roman ruins in the city. A new map. Perhaps on the computer only, so it can have the interactivity."

"I have been trying everywhere to get a map of the sites that were bombed out in 1944 and 1945. *There's* a project for them."

"Why would you want that?"

"Over seven thousand houses were destroyed."

"This was a long time ago."

"I'm not talking about Iuvavum here. The Dom was damaged. At least nobody's hiding that fact. In all, 531 people were killed in the bombing. Just over sixty years ago. Right here. But you can't find out anything about it."

"You found that much out."

"You can't find any details. It's as though it never happened, or it's a story that nobody can seem to remember very well."

"It is hard for you North Americans to understand." With that, she slips away to pee. The bill arrives while she is in the bathroom, and I manage to follow the math, and round up for the tip.

Out in the street she puts an arm around me and nuzzles her face against my chest. I suppose it is her way of saying that nothing is wrong. I like it.

"This one is very famous house," she says, pointing to Pfeifergasse 13.

I see the plaque.

"Here lived Paracelsus when he was first in Salzburg. In fifteen hundreds. He is the patron of my university. You know Paracelsus?"

"The name, of course. Through Jung, mainly. And somebody called Jones. You wouldn't have heard of him."

"It was the bathhouse, too, this place. Paracelsus had his doctor's shop, and his friend had the bathhouse. I think it was here he has come up with his thinking about the weapon salve."

I do not remember the weapon salve from Jung or Jones, so I ask her, more than anything to stretch out the moment. We are standing in front of the house, arms around one another, staring at it as if it has something important to tell us.

"Paracelsus believed the body must heal itself. The physician he can only make the good conditions for that."

"Right. In the chemistry of the disease is found the chemistry of the cure. Didn't he write something like that?"

"Yes. That is very good. You know him then. He was also the poet, and sometimes the magician."

"That's what Jung really liked about him, I think."

"So to cure the wound you have got in battle, he has this fantastic idea. It is very clever. He says you put the salve on the weapon which has done the wounding, and not on the person which is the wounded. It is a very beautiful idea, don't you think?"

"I'll have to think about it."

"It is simple," she says with a giggle, "If I am wounded here" (her eyes) "and here" (her heart), "then I must rub the salve on the weapons that hurt me, like so." She runs her fingers over my cheek and then slips her other hand down the front of my trousers. At that moment, the archeologists start pouring out of Zirkel, and she hurries me off to walk along the river.

WHEN WE WAKE UP in my hotel room, the sun is streaming in. Andrea knows someone with a car she can borrow. "He is just a friend," she assures me, though it hasn't occurred to me to be jealous yet. "We do favours for one another," she adds, which doesn't help. The car is an old Seat. She doesn't see the humour in the name, which is probably because she pronounces it in two syllables. Glad to be rid of my scraped rental car, I don't offer to share the driving. We make a quick stop at her university on the Strubergasse so she can ask a classmate to take notes for her. I turn down the offer of a tour, but can't avoid hearing her explain to her friend that I am a prominent doctor visiting from Canada. At least I think that is what she says. The friend blushes a little and laughs, then shoots me a glance that is unmistakably conspiratorial.

"It is such a fine day. We must go up the mountains, yes?" she asks as we zoom past Christian-Doppler Strasse. "My friend, he does not have the *etikette* for the autobahn in Austria. The sticker. So we go by the smaller roads, through Germany."

"Fine," I say, already feeling a little nauseated from her erratic gear-shifting style. "Will they be wind-y?"

"It is very still today."

"No. Wind-y, winding, you know like a corkscrew?"

"Oh yes! Many windings."

Near Berchtesgaden, she suddenly turns off the main road and begins a very steep climb. On a sharp curve, we barely miss a pedestrian who is heading downhill. He is swinging alpine walking poles and he sports one of those hats with the enormous feather; I am almost sorry that we do not knock the hat off. We reach the hamlet of Obersalzburg and I realize where she is headed: The Intercontinental Hotel, one of the last places on Earth I want to see.

The building itself might be quite pleasing to the eye, if you like stark high modern. And if you don't see in its curved golden stone walls an adoring little brotherness to the Kehlstein House farther up the mountain. To me, it simply looks like a bunker, glorified. It is everything I have read about it in the papers, and more.

Andrea stops the car, pulls the brake, and leaps out to enjoy the view. I cannot move. The car park, according to one article I saw, is on the site of an SS barracks. How can I set my feet there? The golf course we came past is where they blew up the Berghof in the 1950s, eradicating Göring's and Bormann's villas and planting the blasted landscape over with grass and trees. Probably nobody was actually killed here. I know that. It is definitely not the blood-tainted ground of Dachau or Buchenwald. But it is where they thought it all up.

Andrea comes around to my side of the car and reaches for the door handle. I clutch the grip on the arm rest to hold the door shut.

"Is it broken, the door? It is a crappy old Seat. Kurt takes so little care."

I realize then how glad I am it is not an actual Volkswagen, though I think that VW owns Seat now anyway. "I just need a minute."

"I will go and look at the pond." She looks both ways before she crosses the pavement to an ornamental pond and garden. I wonder what cellar, what bunker, has been flooded to make it. But Andrea, at the water's edge now, turns her face back towards me, and I know I must go to her.

"You do not like this place."

I decide to be honest. "I do not like what it was. I do not like what they have made of it now."

"You think they should have left it?"

"I think it should not be so easy to forget some things."

"If here was still the Berghof and the bunkers underneath us, do you think there also would not be people who would come? The new ones, the neo-Nazis, they would make it a shrine. It is better that they blew it up; it is better to cover it up."

"Then why build this place? This should be holy ground."

"Holy ground? Because Hitler and Göring walked on it, and Bormann? Because Speer's office was right over there? The camps, *they* should be holy ground, Daniel, not places like this. It is the *victims* we must remember, do you not think?"

"Then this should be hellish ground. Blocked off. Circled in brimstone. Avoided at all costs. Nobody should be able to stand again where Albert Speer drew up the plans for gas chambers."

"But it is not the mountains' fault. Look how beautiful the view. Nature must finally triumph over history. This is how we think now."

"Hitler chose this place *because* of its nature, because of its geography. Here, on this Bavarian mountain, surrounded by Austria, he could play at being a god in Valhalla. Nature and history are not that easily separated. It *is* the mountains' fault. They are guilty too."

"Why do you hate me?"

"I don't. How could you possibly think —"

"Do you not think that I had grandparents, great-grandparents, too?" she mutters just before we kiss.

The view from the terrace where we have coffee is undeniably spectacular. I tell myself to forget it is nearly the same view that Hitler would have seen on the rare days when his vertigo allowed him to visit the Kehlstein House, looming higher up the mountain behind us. But the coffee leaves a bitter taste in my mouth; hot, and dry.

Andrea drops me at my hotel and lurches off to return the car. The room, which we left a maelstrom of clothes and sheets — a kind of self-conscious monument to our night of lovemaking that I did not like to straighten up — has been tidied by unseen hands. There is a faint whiff of burning, though. I notice that the file folder I had left closed on the desk is now open. The photograph of Mother as a little girl at Kloster Indersdorf should be on top, but it is missing. I follow the smell into the bathroom. In the sink are several delicate flakes of ash, like grey butterfly wings. Who would do such a thing?

Paracelsus tells us that in the burning of any matter the smoke is the mercury, the ghost. The part that has disappeared, that is the sulfur, the spirit. What is left behind, the ash, is the salt, the body.

3. Salt

"I am so sorry, that is quite terrible." Andrea says. "The photograph, it was of your wife?"

I have not told her I was married. I have not told her I am divorced. She has never asked. I no longer wear the ring. "My mother ... as a little girl."

We have met at the bottom of the Linzergasse and are now struggling with the torturous steps that lead off it and up the Kapuzinerberg to the cloister.

"Why would anyone want to burn a picture of your —?"

"It is a picture from 1945. She is holding a card. Her first name is written on the card. It was all they knew about her."

"I see." She stops in front of one of the tableaux

that punctuate the climb. The caption sign has been removed, but it is obviously number four, "Jesus meets his mother." "That is so horrible. Did you tell the *gastgeber*?"

"What if he's the one who did it?"

"Oh."

We continue the climb. Not much farther along, we come across a crouching girl clutching a clipboard and staring intently at the stone wall. Then we meet another, and a pair of boys, all in similar positions, all with clipboards. It must be a school class. Still farther along, some have magnifying glasses and jars.

"Ah, they are hunting for the spiders," announces Andrea. She stops to talk to the young woman who is obviously the teacher. I catch only every sixth word, so Andrea has to interpret for me as we move past them and continue up the mountain. "It is a project to see how many kinds of spiders are on the Kapuzinerberg. They have to capture samples and make charts. It is the science class."

"What will they do with the spiders that they catch, once they have made all their findings?"

"I do not know. I did not ask. I suppose they will not survive in the jars. There is another group that is hunting for spiders on the Nonnberg. I do not know if the teacher meant to make the joke when she said that they expected to find not so many crawly things on the Nun's mountain. That is good, though, don't you think? Not so many crawly things on the Nun's mountain!"

Above the cloister, the mountain is covered with a network of paths that Andrea seems to know as though they are the lines on her palm. She barely hesitates at each new fork before pulling me along. Finally we emerge quite suddenly from the trees and are perched on the edge of a cliff. "Look," she says. "This is the very nicest view of the old town. I love to come here. This is what Mozart would have seen more than two hundred years ago."

"I thought you didn't like Mozart."

"The point is —"

"I know. The point is that it is the same view. No matter what has happened in between."

"Do you not find that this is a comfort?"

"Do you make a habit of leading strange men up mountains to make epiphanies?"

"You are not so strange."

On the way down we do not see the children. Their genetic experiment is over, I suppose. All trace has been erased.

Andrea comes back to the hotel. She says she has an idea. I am embarrassed to hope that it is about sex, and even more embarrassed when I find out it is not.

"We will burn something else. To balance things out."

"That doesn't make any sense. It's irrational. I thought you were a scientist, a medical student."

"It is pure Paracelsus. Fight poison with poison. Just be sure that the dose is exact."

"Are you making that up?"

"I go to his university, remember."

"What exactly were you thinking of burning?"

"It should be another photograph, don't you agree?"

"Am I supposed to go down to the lobby and ask who-ever it was who burned my mother if they have a photo I can borrow?"

"Will this do?" She hands me a small square of folded paper. When I open it out, there is a cross of lines where the coating has worn away at the folds. The image is badly faded, but it is still quite clearly a photograph of an SS officer in full dress, a portrait that might have stood in a silver frame on someone's mantelpiece once.

"Where did you get this?"

"Will it do, do you think?" We go into the bathroom. Andrea instructs me to place the photograph in the sink. "Face up," she says. "He needs to see." Then she sets a match to one corner.

Just as the flame is starting to creep across the photo, there is a knock at the door. I don't know why, but I thrust my hand into the sink to grab the burning paper, as though I am a schoolboy caught at something forbidden. The nerves in my fingers scream at my brain, but I keep holding the thing, waving it around, as if that would put the flame out.

A key turns in the lock. "Allo?" It is a woman's voice.

Andrea gives me a curious look and then rushes to the door, leaving me running cold water over my blis-tering hand and washing the remains of the photo down the drain. I can make out enough of what she and the woman say to one another to know that the woman has brought some towels she had forgotten to leave before, and that Andrea explains to her that I have burned myself and can the woman find any … something I can't quite understand. When the door clicks and Andrea comes back to me, I ask her.

"I have sent her for onions and salt," she explains. "From the kitchen."

"You are hungry?"

"I will make a *salbe*. Crushed onions and salt are good for a burn."

"First-year medicine?"

"*Volks* remedy."

"My mother used to use onions and salt to tell the future."

"She was the fortune teller?"

"Not really the future, I guess. The weather. It was a parlour game, to entertain us children. You cut an onion into twelve wedges and spread them around the table. Each wedge stands for a month. Then you sprinkle salt on them and leave them awhile. The way the salt and the piece of onion react tells you something about what the weather will be in that month. How much moisture."

Hours later, the room smells of onions and sex. I have surprised myself at what I can still manage with one hand. Andrea comes back from the bathroom. She has had a shower and she looks, with her hair slicked back, just as she did the first time I saw her.

"You didn't get yourself completely dry."

"It is hot in the bathroom. I am sweating."

I reach for the sheet and begin dabbing at her.

"Thank you. My breasts were weeping. You have dried their tears."

"You just don't know how to use a towel."

"It is tears and sweat. Taste."

She is right, of course. And in the salt on her skin I taste her blood.

OUR SECOND TRIP OF the day to the Linzergasse takes us to the church of St. Sebastian. On the way, I tell her a joke that I remember about Zeno's paradox and St. Sebastian. If Zeno is right, the joke goes, and an arrow shot from a bow covers half the distance to its target and then half that distance and half that distance, and so on, then St. Sebastian can only have died of fright.

"I do not understand."

"St. Sebastian was the one who was filled full of arrows, right?"

"Of course."

"But if the arrow can never reach its target, like Zeno suggests, then ..."

"But he *is* filled with arrows, you said so yourself."

"It's just a joke."

"Without his arrows, St. Sebastian would mean nothing."

We arrive at the church, despite Zeno.

It is actually the *friedhof* she wants to show me, the cemetery. We start with the tomb of Mozart's widow.

"I thought you hated Mozart."

"Read the stone."

"Constanze Nissen. Nissen, that was the name of the man she married after Mozart died?"

"He is not so famous, but he was making her very happy. Most people do not remember his name. But that is not the main thing. Look about when she was born."

I read out the year 1763, and Freyburg.

"Now look down below."

There is a small slab applied to the bottom of the stone that reads: *Recte: geboren 5 January 1762 Zell im Wiesental*. "They made a mistake?"

"It is how it seems. Yes."

"But why not just fix the original inscription? Why leave the wrong information there on the stone and also go to all the trouble of cutting a new stone to correct it a few inches down below?"

"What if the correction itself is wrong? Sometimes we do not help things just to cover them up. I thought this would interest you."

She leads me in a circle around Wolf Dietrich's mausoleum that serves as the centrepiece of the *friedhof*, and then to the church door. There, in an alcove, stands the sepulchre of Paracelsus. The tablet explains that the remains of the great alchemist were dug up and reinterred here when the church was renovated in 1752.

"He was moved one other time before that, too, in 1572 — all the same numerals, isn't that strange? This was when they wanted to build a new chapel just where he was buried. It was not exactly the resurrection he had foreseen, I think. And then for them to dig him up again almost two hundred years later, it must have been —"

"This is a place of honour, though. More holy. It does more honour to his bones to be here just at the church door, doesn't it?"

"It is what they thought. In 1752 when they put him here, they even had a likeness painted for the door of the sepulchre. It stood there, where you see this bas-relief now. The sculpture replaced the painting at a later time."

"The marble is more lasting."

"It was not that. The painting was a mistake. It was a likeness of his father, not of Paracelsus."

"Poor bastard. So many indignities. But at least they eradicated the mistake, not like poor Constanze's birthdate."

"Yes, they covered it over. No one would ever know to look. How lucky for him, do you not think?"

"Don't think I am going to start saying that everything should be whitewashed over."

"There is a story that Paracelsus wanted to be cut into quarters and buried in shit."

"I had no idea he was so self-loathing. The way that Jung presents him —"

"He is supposed to have hoped to spring to life again that way. There is another story that he grew a little man."

"The infamous homunculus. Right."

"You have heard of this?"

"How Paracelsus is supposed to have grown a little

man out of a handful of semen steeped in horse manure? Yes. It's one of those stories people love to tell to —"

"Nothing stays in the state that it is in. That is what Paracelsus tells us, Daniel. And that life … life grows out of decay." She does not add what I expect her to: that some traces are better removed, some things better forgotten. I suppose she left that argument on the mountain.

FOR DINNER, WE DECIDE to return to the Zirkel. There are no archeologists tonight, and we sit downstairs where the smoke seems a little less thick. Andrea is quiet but hungry. Only when her plate is empty does she begin to talk.

"Do you think it is possible to make real change, Daniel?"

"I am a psychiatrist, remember? I think you have a joke on the subject, something about a light bulb."

"The food we just ate. It is being changed right now. Really changed."

"Into shit you mean?"

"Just like we are the alchemist. Transforming it. Turning it into something new."

"It's not quite on the same level with making gold with the philosopher's stone."

"We grow hair not because there is hair in our food. There is not nails to grow nails, or muscles … well, perhaps muscles, but … it is a kind of miracle. Also that we do not grow to look like what we eat. You would be a large breast of the turkey."

Before heading for the river we stop again in front of Pfeifergasse 13.

"What are you thinking?" I ask her.

"I am making the little prayer. To the man who gave us the elements."

"Earth, air, fire, water? Like in the Mirabell Gardens?"

"You know I do not mean those."

"Sorry. Sulfur, Mercury, Salt. That's what your friend Paracelsus would have said, isn't it?"

"The Arabs already knew the first two. He only added salt."

"You make it sound like a cooking class. But he didn't mean actual salt."

"For him they were all principles."

"Tendencies."

"*Genau*. Like the Father, the Son, and the Holy Ghost. Sulfur is the Father; mercury is the Holy Ghost. Salt is the Son — the flesh: the body. One time, he wrote: 'without salt no part of the body could be grasped.' I like the sound of this, don't you?" The last time we stood here she would have touched me, grasped me somewhere, to demonstrate.

"The body is also ash. Isn't that right?"

"What is left behind after the alchemy is all done."

"Where did you get that photograph that we burned this afternoon?"

"It was a very old photograph."

"Where did you get it?"

"It belonged to my father."

"Where did he —?"

"It is a portrait of his grandfather."

"Jesus."

"I do not think so."

"What do you know about him?"

"Why would I want to know anything about him? You are hurting —"

"What do you —?"

"His name was Andreas Wendl. He was officer in the SS."

"That part is obvious from the picture."

"At the end of the war, in the last days, he returned again into his town. Nobody spoke of these things. Life went on. You cannot understand."

"Where was his town?"

"It was near here. On the German side. On the river too. But he was far away for most of the war."

"Where was his town? The one he came back to at the end of the war?"

"It is called Laufen. Have you heard of it?"

I don't know what I expect to happen. That the earth should open up, at least. That the graves across the Salzach in St. Sebastian's churchyard should vomit forth their dead. That some wound in me should bleed afresh in the presence of the great-granddaughter of a man who might have been my mother's jailer.

Instead, there is only silence. Even the traffic along Rudolfskai has stopped, it seems. And then amid the silence I hear Andrea weep.

I lean in to wipe the tears, their brine sticky on my fingers. I take her hand. The past, I realize in this moment, can be only mercury, only sulfur. This hand between my palms is all there is, all we have, here, now: the body, solid, ash, salt.

We walk towards the river that flows on from here past the place where my mother was finally free to run.

Ageusia

One

I realize now that it started to fall apart on the night of the wine tasting. Antoine was practising his patter on his sister Sherry and her boyfriend and me. The community college wanted him to do a quick-and-easy tutorial for their first-year restaurateur's course. Since he refuses to present any dish in public before trying it out on family first, we were being lectured at about wine. He had covered colour and clarity and was moving on to taste.

"Your tongue can only register four sensations: sweet, sour, bitter, and salt."

"What about umami?" asked Sherry.

"What's that?"

"This new one they talk about. Like tasting MSG or protein or something."

"We don't bother with that." Antoine was obviously

a little annoyed at the interruption. I wondered how he would ever cope with teaching. "And we don't bother with salt, since it's unlikely that a wine will actually taste salty. So that narrows the tastes down to three. Each one is sensed on a different part of the tongue."

"That sounds simple enough." I was trying to be supportive. "And threes are easy for people to remember. Students retain threes easily." I couldn't resist reminding him that I am a teacher all of the time, not just by invitation. "So, there's sweet, sour, and bitter."

"I was reading this thing the other day about the evolutionary advantages of the sense of taste." Sherry is always reading and always wanting to talk about it. It drives Antoine crazy, but she is his only sister and much younger, so he puts up with it. "It was all about the sweetness of mother's milk and the sourness of pee and how being able to distinguish between the two is a helpful thing for a baby's survival. Obvious, I guess, but clever."

"But it's a lot more complex than just telling those three sensations apart, isn't it Antoine? Wine tasting, I mean." Matt was one of those good boyfriends who can negotiate a peace between siblings without managing to upset either.

Antoine thanked him with a look and continued. "Smell is what complicates it. Or should I say that smell is what makes it gloriously interesting?"

"I think the second one," I said. "It sounds more glass-is-half-full."

"Speaking of which, are you going to be allowed to

actually pour wine for them all? What if some of them aren't nineteen? It *is* a community college."

"Do you *have* to be of legal age to swish and spit?"

"What is it about smell, Antoine? Tell us." I could see he was about to give up on us altogether if he wasn't allowed to go on with his notes.

"The nose can distinguish something like five thousand different smells. Most of the time when we are tasting something we're also actually smelling it, so you can see that once you add smell into the mix, the possibilities multiply."

"Five thousand is a lot," I said, as though he is himself responsible for the subtlety of the human nose.

"It is. We can't possibly give each smell its own name, of course. So we often simply say that one thing smells like another."

"Like cum smells like Chlorox." Sherry surprised even Matt with this outburst.

"And people do the same thing with wine," I said, to steer things in a safer direction. "That's why you might say there's a hint of peach, for example, in a white, even though peaches never went within a hundred metres of the wine?"

"Exactly."

"So the tongue is just ... Oh. Sorry, Antoine, go on with your notes. It's very interesting."

"The tongue is just what?" Sherry asked me.

"It's okay. I can wait. I want to hear what Antoine has to say."

But while he went on to list three or four dozen common likenesses to look for (vanilla, lemon, blackberry, leather ...), I started to drift. It was only when Matt sneezed violently that I realized I had not been paying attention.

"Bless you."

"Red wine always makes me do that."

"Histamines."

"I thought it was pheromones. I do the same thing with gin."

"*And* he sneezes when he thinks he's about to get sex. That's what makes him think it has to be pheromones. Exactly the same sneezes. Actually, there's no proof that humans even communicate with pheromones."

"Tell that to the perfume industry." Matt is doing an MBA in Marketing.

"No, it's true. There's no anatomical evidence of a functioning Jacobson's organ by the time a fetus has reached full term. That's the thing that picks up pheromones, the vomeronasal organ. I don't know who Jacobson was. Lots of animals are born with them, but with us they've disappeared by the time we're breathing air."

"Maybe mine's still intact."

Antoine gave up on his prepared talk, with remarkably good humour. "Where is this little organ supposed to be exactly, Sherry? In those animals that have it?"

"It's kind of halfway between the nose and the mouth. It could provide the perfect explanation for taste being dependent on smell. Kind of a mixing bowl. Only it doesn't exist. Except maybe in Matt." Sherry kissed Matt, which made him sneeze again.

"What were you going to say about the tongue, Claire?"

"I've almost forgotten. Just something about how, if I'm understanding any of this, the tongue itself really only makes a purely mechanical response to stimuli, sending pretty simple messages about sweet or sour or bitter or salt."

"And maybe umami."

"But that's not what taste really is, in the end, is it? That's what you're saying. It's much more, I don't know, imaginative. Poetic. You know, how you said we draw on our sense of smell to make all those metaphors or similes or whatever."

"You mean when something sweet touches your tongue all the taste buds signal is just that, end of story: there's something sweet here, they say. So then something else has to happen for it to be tasted as sweet like honey as distinct from sweet like, say, glucose water? I'm not sure whether there are data to back that up."

Thanks to Sherry's biweekly stints in Dr. Morton's lab, her vocabulary had become larded with pseudo-scientific terms. Antoine and I had laughed about it before. I turned back to him: "So, you're going to talk to them about the eye, the mouth, and the nose. Is that the basic shape of the lesson? Sounds great. Threes again."

"I thought I would say something about the great wine-growing regions too. Or do you think that would be too much?"

"They'll be expecting it, won't they? I mean, it's an essential part of being a wine snob, isn't it? Oh, relax, Antoine, I mean snob in the nicest possible way: connoisseur, really." His sister patted his hand in a decidedly motherly way.

"Why *is* that anyway? Does it really matter if a person knows where in the world a wine comes from? Are we so much wiser about wine than the ancient Greeks were? They only knew the wines from their own little hillsides or whatever." I saw Antoine wince when I said it, but I ploughed on anyway. "Sometimes I think life was simpler, better, when a person only lived in one little part of the world."

"I know what you're saying, Claire," said Sherry, who almost certainly didn't. "But I'm not sure you can compare the evils of economic globalization with the simple ability to tell a Côtes du Rhône from a Côtes du Beaune."

I didn't bother to say that I was actually thinking more about boys from the St. John River Valley dying in Afghanistan. That was a stupid comparison too, I knew. I couldn't get those dead soldiers out of my head.

Antoine produced a Chilean Cabernet Sauvignon and poured us each a mouthful. I tried to swirl it the way the others were doing, to see its legs, its tears, its cathedral windows. Then I tried to concentrate hard on the interplay between my tongue and my nose.

"A little of the barnyard," Antoine pronounced. "Leather."

"Exactly," Sherry and Matt chimed in.

"I don't get leather."

"Just for an instant. Couldn't you? It's like a little tang of salt."

"I thought you said that wine couldn't be salty."

"There's definitely leather there."

"I don't taste it."

"Three of us do. Try again."

"I'm fine, actually. I'm sure you're right." Unbelievably, he was always appeased by this kind of apparent compliance, no matter how snide my tone. I, on the other hand, seethed for the rest of the evening.

Two

The thing about having a chef as a lover is the things he can do with his mouth. I don't mean the kissing and all those other kinds of attention, though Antoine was remarkably good at all of that too. It's the awareness, the sensitivity, that is uncanny. A chef can detect more with his mouth than most guys can with all of their other senses combined, including their common sense. This makes him very hard to hide anything from, which is fine most of the time. I'm all for honesty. Just not as an utterly unbreakable principle.

"Something is wrong, Claire."

I felt his erection deflate, like dough when something kills the yeast. I knew I would not be able to escape
talking about it. Just the same, I tried to stall. "I'm probably a little tired, but I do want to be doing this. Really.
What can I do to make it more interesting for you?"

"There is something different about you."

"I'm trying a new shampoo."

"You also haven't shaved your armpits for more than
a week, but that's not it. It's when we're kissing."

"I told you, I'm tired."

"Your mouth seems drier."

"Drier than what?" I knew this wouldn't work. He
hated this kind of game. But it bought me a little time
to think while he sighed and shook his head. I had no
response prepared because I'd never imagined that
a person could actually sense another person's dry
mouth. I'm not sure why I was so reluctant to tell him
I'd been taking amitriptyline for the past month. Lots
of people take things for depression. It's almost unusual
not to, these days, with the world in the state it's in.
And it was certainly not as though he was the one who
had driven me to it. "I think I might have been sleeping
with my mouth open a lot." This was not a direct lie.
It was in a perfectly true statement. If he made a false
connection and chose to interpret it as an explanation
for the dry mouth, that was his business.

"But your mouth wouldn't stay dry, not after you
woke up, not after you'd had it shut for a bit, would it?"

"I don't know. Would it?" I drew circles around

his nipples with my index finger, but he was not to be distracted.

"I don't remember seeing you sleep with your mouth open."

"You're asleep when I do it."

"How do you know?"

"Are you hungry?" It was my final card. I hated to play it too often. When your lover is a chef, you can gain a lot of weight.

"A little. Actually, I have something I want you to try. I'll be right back."

I stayed in bed, watching him cross the room, loving the deep dimples in the sides of his bum, wishing I had told him the truth. He was out the door before I whispered, "It's a side effect of some medication I'm on." Then I heard him rummaging in a kitchen drawer, opening a cupboard, the clatter of a plate. And he was back. Obviously, it was not going to be a hot entrée.

"You'll love this. I discovered it by accident the other day." He put a plate on the duvet between us. There was a bar of dark chocolate centred on it.

"Where did you discover it? At the checkout at Sobey's? My people call this a chocolate bar. A cho-co-late bar. Very nice, but not haute cuisine, sweetie."

"Try a piece."

I took a bite. "Okay, so it's obviously not from the grocery store. But it's still essentially a chocolate bar, right?"

He produced a small cylindrical container, not quite

the size of two hockey pucks stacked on one another. There was a paper seal, which he broke with his fingernail before prying off the cork top.

"What's that?"

"Fleur de sel."

"Part of The Collection?" We always capitalized the initials when we spoke of it. Antoine had been developing the idea of marketing "salts of the globe" as a kind of sideline to the restaurant. Matt was helping him with it.

He nodded and took a pinch between his fingers, letting it fall into his palm so I could have a look. The grains were large, mostly irregular, not a brilliant white, but certainly not grey like some of the Guérande stuff he had shown me before.

"Take another bite of the chocolate."

He didn't have to ask me twice.

"Now, try it with this." He crumbled the fleur de sel over a piece he had broken off the bar.

"Can I swallow this first?"

"Sorry. Of course. It's just such an amazing sensation. I'm eager for you to try."

"Okay. Here goes." I took the piece of chocolate from him and popped it in my mouth. It tasted exactly like the last one. "That *is* amazing."

"You wouldn't have thought of it, would you?"

"I don't think I would."

"Mixing the two."

"And how the salt disappears completely."

"What?"

"The fleur de sel. It has no taste. What is it? Does some-thing in the chocolate neutralize it or something?"

Antoine looked at me for a second and then pinched some more salt onto the remains of the bar of chocolate before putting it all into his mouth at once. He chewed a while before saying: "You were kidding, right? Making a joke."

"No. I really couldn't tell the difference."

He took another few grains between his thumb and forefinger and pushed them into my mouth, a kind of forced penetration.

I could feel the flakes of fleur de sel. I crunched them with my teeth. But there was no flavour. And that was when I realized I had a problem.

Three

My friend Liz is also a colleague, although we usually try to keep our lunches social. Sometimes, however, it's hard to separate the two relationships. Usually, we met at Antoine's restaurant, but whenever I needed to talk about my love life we needed to go somewhere else. The food was never as good.

"So he was really upset?"

"It was as though I had stabbed him right through the heart. Like I was suddenly some kind of a monster, certainly less of a woman."

"What difference could it possibly make to him? It's not like you're suddenly frigid or something."

"I *have* been less interested lately, actually. I put it down to the depression. Or the pills I'm taking for it."

"But this thing with your taste buds. What did you call it?"

"Ageusia. Technically, it's hypogeusia when you just lose some sensation, I guess. It's only salt I can't taste."

"How can that affect your sex life? Or his?"

"He's a chef. How can he stay with a girlfriend who can't taste properly?"

"Bury yourself in your teaching. That's what I do. And your research. What are you working on?"

Liz is a Jane Austen person, surprisingly productive considering that everything that can usefully be said about Gentle Jane has to have been written by now. I always feel inadequate describing my own efforts. "It's Grimm, actually."

"It can't be that bad." We both knew she had to say it. "Okay, seriously, what are you doing with old Jacob now?" I had been trying unsuccessfully to come up with something respectable to do with Grimm for months. She knew this, but she asked anyway. It's what colleagues do.

"I am thinking about something to do with severed body parts. You know, when somebody chops off somebody's ring finger and it eventually comes back to point to them as a murderer."

"The Robber Bridegroom." One of the reasons why I try not to talk shop with Liz is that she always has to know as much as I do about anything, even my own specialty.

"Among others."

"The robber-murderers chop off a dead girl's finger when her ring won't come off easily, and the finger flies away and ends up in the bosom of the bride-to-be as she lies hidden and watching them. Right?"

"Something like that." It was exactly like that.

"Wow. You can have a field day with that. Especially if you were a Freudian, I suppose. That's also the one where she scatters peas along her route into the woods, even though the bridegroom has already marked it with ashes, right? When the ashes blow away, she is able to find her way back by following where the peas have sprouted. And lentils too, isn't it? What do you think the lentils mean?"

"I'm only interested in the finger."

"I wonder. What happens to the murdered girl while the bride-to-be watches from her hiding place? Besides their cutting off her finger, I mean?"

"They tear off her delicate raiment."

"Right, of course; they always do that. Boys. And then?"

"Then they put her on a table and cut her beautiful body in pieces and boil her up in a cauldron."

"You're forgetting one detail, aren't you?"

"Oh my God. Of course. They sprinkle her with salt. You don't think I'm —?"

"How well do you know Antoine? He does have some mighty big pots, doesn't he? And then there's that salt collection you've told me about."

I let Liz think she had managed to explain my symptoms through some kind of mythopoetic process, like I was a piece of literature; and we moved on to talk of other things.

Four

Even before I had shut the door behind me that night, Antoine was trying to get me to sit down on the couch. I asked him why he wasn't at the restaurant. He said he had more important things to do. Like this. Since he wasn't letting me take my coat off, I gathered that "this" was not sex, though I was a little frightened for a moment when I glimpsed a shiny English cucumber on the coffee table. Maybe I should have strewn lentils along my path.

"I have a new salt I want you to try."

I wished then he would just cut me up and stuff me in a kettle. This must be like the pressure men feel when they have erectile dysfunction, I thought.

"It's from the Himalayas. They say it's the oldest salt on earth. And it's pink, which is kind of fun." He made it sound like he was offering me something in a shade of blushing rose from Victoria's Secret. I wanted to tell him I had a headache.

"Antoine, I —"

"Sorry. Am I going too fast? Would you like a drink?"

"No let's get this over with." This was of course the wrong thing to say and it took several minutes for me to manage to coax him to produce this latest find.

It was indeed pink. It was also in rock form, the size of a walnut shell.

"Am I supposed to suck on it?"

He fished a small metal grater out of his pocket. Who carries a grater around in his pants? "It comes from ancient seas. Before there was pollution. Before there were people to make the pollution."

I was not sure why this was supposed to be so appealing. Did he think my problem was that I had become resistant to the more recently evaporated salts because they're so full of toxins? Like I was making some kind of ecological protest.

"The mine is called Khewra. It was discovered nearly twenty-four hundred years ago. In the time of Alexander the Great. Since the nineteenth century, they have been mining it on the Dr. Warth principle."

"You're making this up. What's the Dr. Warth principle?"

"You mine only fifty per cent and leave the other fifty per cent to hold the mine up. It's all written up on the label. I'll cut the blurb down a bit for The Collection."

"By about fifty per cent?"

He sliced the cucumber onto a plate, then, seeing my look, explained. "It's what we call a tasting medium."

"I like chocolate better."

"Not for this." What he meant to say was if I couldn't taste the salt there wouldn't be any consolation prize this time, no alternative sensation to be had.

When he held the grater above the cucumbers and started rubbing the chunk against it, I found myself wondering what Liz would have had to say about the significance of this little episode. Would she have gone for the obvious grating-on-my-nerves interpretation, or would she have opted for something more sexual? I decided I would not report to her. Friends don't need to share everything.

The cucumber slices began to sweat immediately. I knew how they felt. I considered faking it, saying my God, yes, isn't that fantastic and so forth. But I knew he would be able to tell, and I didn't think he deserved to be lied to about this.

"Have you tried it?" I asked, sounding like some ancient queen with her royal taster. There was a remote chance that he could decide the salt was inferior, not worth my while; and I was willing to take that chance.

"I am not the one with the ..." But he stopped, picked up a slice of cucumber jewelled in pink salt and slid it between his lips. His eyes closed to help him concentrate. I considered scraping the salt off a slice while he wasn't looking, but realized that would accomplish nothing. It wasn't that I couldn't tolerate salt; it was only that I could not taste it. Eating an unsalted slice of cucumber would be no better than eating a salted one, for a person with my condition. "Exquisite," he pronounced. Oh great.

"Maybe if I shut my eyes. You could feed it to me. Do you remember that scene in *Tom Jones*? The movie, not the book, I mean. Maybe it's in the book too." I swung my feet up on the couch and leaned back a little on the arm, closing my eyes. He trailed his fingers up my shin to the knee. I could feel the goosebumps rising. Then he continued up the inner surface of my thigh, burrowing beneath my skirt. Usually I flinched when his fingers reached the leg band of my underpants, but this time I warned myself not to and instead made a tiny sigh, hoping to distract him from the salt test, however temporarily. But his other hand was at my mouth, posting a cucumber slice between my lips like it was a letter.

The cucumber was lovely and fresh, with hints of grass and tea and even a touch of honey. And I could certainly feel the salt, gritty, threatening, daring me to taste an ocean millions of years gone dry. But of course, I couldn't.

Five

The weekend away was my idea. I had been in enough relationships to know the signs of real trouble. I hoped if we could just change the context for a little while, maybe everything would go back the way it was. My shrink friend, Daniel, who had been helping me a little on the side with the depression, had a theory that my problems with tasting might be a quite natural expression of a loss of sexual interest. He quoted Ernest Jones and all kinds of disgusting theories about the significance of salt. Although I neither agreed nor disagreed with him to his face, since it was really none of his business how Antoine and I got on in the bedroom, the connection seemed plausible. The tasting problem came up at about the same time my physical feelings for Antoine changed. I was just not sure which was the chicken and which the egg.

On the way down the coast, I made the mistake of turning on the car radio. More news of fresh disasters, as somebody used to say. Suicide bombings, mortar attacks, even a typhoon — all in places we hear about these days as if they are just around the corner. I went to switch the station and Antoine nearly went off the road. "Leave it," he barked. "I want to hear." So we hurtled along the highway with its stunning views of the Bay of Fundy while our minds were locked on the suffering in far-flung places we would never see.

When the newscast ended, he switched the radio off. "Sorry if I was a little sharp," he said. "I just think we owe it to them to listen."

"Owe it to them?"

"As a kind of sign of respect. Of empathy maybe. For all those poor people and what they go through."

I put a CD in and we listened to Norah Jones for the rest of the ride.

ANTOINE HAD NEVER STAYED at the hotel, although he had eaten in the dining room often enough because the chef is a friend. I had asked for a room in the old part, and his reaction was everything I hoped for. "It's like a fly in amber. I bet there isn't another place quite like it on earth. You can feel just what people must have felt when they came here when the place was new, can't you? I love it."

We had to work quite hard to figure out the brass mechanism that opened the French doors. Flakes of paint grated off and fell like snow on the hardwood floor. There was no balcony; just a screen with a railing. The formality of the gardens was broken by the brightly coloured wooden chairs sprinkled around the lawns. If you squinted, you could easily imagine ladies in long white dresses with parasols and gentlemen with straw boaters, here for a month of retreat from the pressures of Montreal or Toronto, in a simpler, more civilized time.

We made love on the floor with the curtains open and blowing in the breeze. I was pretty sure the sightlines were okay and that nobody looking up from shuffleboard would see us naked. Maybe just my feet at one point. I don't know what Antoine was thinking about, but I imagined us as a pair of Edwardian lovers who only met once a year when our families packed themselves on the train and came to the seaside for a holiday. I bit on the sleeve of my cast-off shirt so as not to make too much noise. We were both glad to be here, I thought, as we finished. It was a good idea.

By late afternoon the breeze off the bay had freshened. We walked down into the town under the canopy of old trees and between rows of even older houses. The wharf was crawling with tourists fresh off a whale-watching boat, but we found a bench and sat for a few minutes in the kind of silence that all lovers hope for.

"There's nothing like it," said Antoine finally, taking a deep breath, pulling the air down into his lungs. "That smell."

I mimicked his breath and nodded. "Salt air. Salt water."

"You can smell it?"

Why couldn't he leave it alone?

"Describe it. What does it smell like?"

"There's nothing wrong with my — Like seaweed. Like mud. Like summer."

"That's what I smell too. Exactly what I smell."

I guess this was supposed to make me feel good, to reforge a bond between us that had been missing ever since I couldn't taste the leather in that Cabernet Sauvignon, so I took his hand and kissed it. I didn't point out that what we were smelling was the air or the water or both. Salt, in and of itself, has no smell, not for anyone. It is for the tongue alone. I had been reading up.

Back in the room, he got out his notes on Salts of the Globe and went to turn on the television. I reminded him how that would spoil the illusion. What he said he liked about the place was its evocation of a different era.

I suggested we try shuffleboard or see if they would rent us some tennis racquets, but it was six o'clock and he had to see the news. Didn't I want to know what's going on in the big world? he asked. I slipped out after the headlines, and took my book down to one of the timeless wooden lawn chairs.

Six

Antoine and I almost never gave dinner parties. For him, he said, it would be like asking Matisse to paint your bathroom, which I used to think was insulting until I remembered how much I hate being asked to read pages of bad poetry written by the fragile daughters of old friends. Our compromise was a kind of face-saving fiction: that he was giving me "cooking lessons" while I prepared all of the food. When I was lucky, he got impatient and took over and did it all anyway. The dinner party I had planned for four of my colleagues was not one of those lucky occasions. His patience as I muddled around the kitchen trying to follow instructions would have put Job to shame. That would have been a heart-warming show of support if I hadn't known it was actually intended to punish me.

We somehow got into a discussion about kosher salt — probably because George, the new guy in my department, was Jewish, however non-observant.

"How is it kosher?"

"Well, it's not, really. That is, I guess that it qualifies technically. Lots of things do."

"Don't they have to be blessed by a rabbi?"

"That's a myth. They have to be produced in a certain way and be not on various lists of prohibited foods. That's all."

"You aren't answering my question. Why call it kosher if it doesn't matter? Or why not call lots of other things kosher too?"

"It's really kosher*ing* salt. They rake it constantly to produce a certain kind of grain. The size of the grains make it excellent for drawing out moisture ... well, blood, in particular."

"Then it should be *called* koshering salt. That might be less off-putting. Less exclusive."

"Do you think?"

"I always thought I shouldn't be using it. Like I didn't have the right. Anyway, it disappears just like any other salt," I said, tossing a small handful into some water I had boiling for a zucchini we were going to have cold in the salad. "It *is* okay to use it in boiling water?" He was always adamant that specialty salts should not be wasted in this way, but I didn't think the kosher, the kosher*ing,* salt counted.

Most of the menu had to be done at the last minute, which meant it was one of those parties where the guests could either entertain themselves in the living room or hang around the kitchen watching the hosts quarrel. Since they were my colleagues and the party was my idea,

Antoine insisted on the latter. He brought chairs from the dining room for them.

"Claire is a nervous cook. It will be good for her to have an audience," he said.

"I can't even boil water," said Liz, which I knew wasn't true, but I was grateful for the support.

"Do you keep kosher?" asked George, looking suspiciously at our dishes. Then he laughed, thank God, and said: "Good. Me neither."

"We have some salt you'll like," said Antoine.

Enid, who likes to interview people rather than talk to them, asked Antoine about his latest project. "Claire tells me you're about to market a collection of salts. How ever did you come up with that idea?"

"People in the restaurant were always asking me about the salts I was using to finish dishes. I thought there must be an interest there. And we live in a global village now, don't we?"

"Do we?" Peter has to question everything. He thinks he's being Socratic.

Antoine seemed at a loss for an answer.

"Perhaps the idea of a global village is really just the new imperialism?"

"Like salt is the new pepper?" I couldn't resist.

"I'm serious," said Peter. He always is. "Think about the British Empire and its policies on salt."

We all thought, but nobody had anything to say. Maybe, like me, they had no idea about the Empire's salt policy.

"It's what drove Gandhi to rebellion. Partly. Remember

the march to the sea? How by picking up a crust of evaporated salt he broke the British Salt law and set off a string of other protests? That was all about producing locally, living where you live, not having another country's salt forced on you."

"I hardly think that Antoine's new enterprise is forcing foreign salt on people." Enid always disagrees with Peter even when she thinks he's right.

"What are we sampling tonight?" asked Liz, trying to defuse whatever situation she thought might be arising.

"A little from two of the other oceans. Nothing Indian tonight, I'm afraid, Peter."

"But something vaguely Arthurian for Enid," I said. Enid is our medievalist and a Camelot nut. When Antoine looked puzzled I continued: "The *Halen Môn*. It's from the Isle of Anglesey."

"I thought Arthur was Cornwall."

"The smart money is on North Wales, now," said Enid. I passed her the blue cardboard cylinder and she read us the Welsh. It sounded right, but none of us would know. "*Pur Gwyn*," she read, "that means pure white. *Gwyn* means white. Like Guinevere. Pure. Virginal."

"What version of that story are you reading?" asked Peter. "Besides, everybody knows that salt and libido are directly linked. The taste for one and the taste for the other, you can't separate them."

"What are you serving this Welsh salt with?" asked Liz, once again showing why she should be our next department chair.

"Slow-roasted cherry tomatoes, in fact."

"Help me to salt, help me to sorrow," sighed George who has had a few poems published recently and enjoys making bardic pronouncements.

"So the Welsh salt is the Atlantic. And what's the other?"

"Black lava from Hawaii."

"Sounds like a Greek dessert."

"No. Black lava."

"Is it actually black? How can salt be black?"

"How can *Gwyn* be pure?"

"They dry it with lava rock. It takes on the colour. And some of the minerals. Claire will be serving it on scallops. It's a beautiful look."

"Local scallops?" asked Peter.

"Of course. Sea ones, the big ones."

"I think this Salts of the Globe idea is going to be a big success, Antoine. Hawaiian salt on Bay of Fundy scallops. Wow. It doesn't get more global village than that. It's a natural."

"Like teenaged boys getting blown up by landmines away over in Afghanistan when they should just be fishing shad up the river here." I couldn't help myself. It just came out. "Actually," I said, daring Antoine to challenge me, "there's a change of plan. We'll have the scallops just as they are, and you can choose to salt your tomatoes or not."

Seven

Liz and I have met at the market for lunch. We are pretending to look at one of the gourmet food stands while we make up our minds where to eat. We both know we won't decide until we have given this other issue a thorough airing.

"You moved out? Just like that?"

"It's over. You saw how things were by the end of the dinner party."

"He was drunk. We were all a little drunk."

"I'm not blaming him. It's me, I think. The way I am right now. He'll be fine. He has the restaurant, and The Collection to launch."

"Maybe you should up your dosage?"

"Maybe the medication is the problem. Actually I'm tapering off it."

"Maybe the world is the problem. The way you're relating to it."

It's amazing the things that some people will say just as you're standing looking at a jar of almond-stuffed olives. It might have taken a therapist two years to work up to this diagnosis, and Liz simply puts it out there without any preamble.

"It is a pretty fucked-up world."

"It always was. We just didn't know as much, or as fast."

"But now that we do …"

"Learn to take it with a grain of —" She breaks off too late.

But something has caught my eye as she spoke. The packaging is plain cellophane with a label affixed. There's a map of Nova Scotia with a star where Guysborough County is, and, off the coast, a woodcut of a man and a woman raking something. I pick it up, feeling the coarse grains beneath the cellophane, and read the sticker on the back: "Moonlight Island Sea Salts are harvested in the old traditional ways popular in Europe for centuries. These salts carry valuable mineral traces vital for health. Moonlight Island Sea Salts — a little taste of Europe from Nova Scotia." Jesus. "I want fish and chips," I tell Liz. "Lord's. Now."

While we wait for the woman to load our orders onto their cardboard boats, Liz and I stock our trays with ketchup and vinegar. I take pepper; she takes both. Everything used to be in pumps and shakers but now it's in those little individual pouches. Except the salt. It comes in paper if you want it that way, but there is still the dented metal shaker that's been there forever, the one with the handle like on a mug. Just before we head to our table, I pick this up and shake it over my food, for nostalgia as much as anything. Habit.

"God, there is nothing like this fish, is there?" Liz is saying. "It's like they just caught it, which they probably did."

But I am not listening to her. I have taken one bite and headed straight back to the counter. There is a man trying to decide between the light lunch and the regular fish and chips, but I interrupt him. "Your salt," I say, holding up the dull grey shaker. "Where does it come from?"

The woman stares for a minute and then probably decides it's safer to humour me. She produces a box from a shelf behind her, hands it across the counter.

It is plain Windsor. Ordinary table salt. From Pugwash, fifty kilometres from where I was born. I race back to our table to tell Liz. You see, the thing is that I can taste it; I can actually taste it.

Mann im salz

One

He stands at the back of the church because it is easier to feel God there. Standing at the back, he can look around freely, drink in the beauty of the high vaulted ceiling, study the rococo statuary. In the pews, the traffic can become unbearable. Tourists drop in and out without any regard for where the celebrant might be in his journey through the Mass. He has seen what can happen when these visitors suddenly decide they have had enough Mozart and want to move on to taste another of Salzburg's charms. Once, a devout lady in a dirndl, whose family had probably been sitting in the same pew for centuries, flatly refused to move to allow a family of Americans to get out after the *Agnus Dei*. The Americans had looked around, considered their options, and decided to climb over the immovable worshipper — one more alp to be conquered. They had

193

managed to make it to the aisle, but not without several pinches and at least one bone-crunching kick. Where Siegfried stands, there is no danger of such international incidents. And he has never had to move a centimetre for a tourist.

Today, the choir is singing Mozart's Sparrow Mass, both *brevis* and *solemnis*, in C. He would have been here anyway. He has not missed a Sunday in the *Peterskirche* since he began his job on the *bergbahn* two years ago. But his piety feels especially rewarded on the days when the music is so perfectly to his taste. With this Mass, there is the added pleasure of knowing that the most complete set of original parts sits not fifty metres away, in the church archives. The annotations are in the composer's own hand. The *echtheit* of it excites him; he always likes to know that he is in touch with something absolutely genuine. It is how he was brought up. He loves to think he can feel the direct line from Mozart's pen to his ear.

The orchestra is made up of players who are contracted individually for each occasion. He had a drink once with the *musik direktor* who told him all about the arrangements as if it was what you usually discussed over a Stiegl. Many of them are still students at the Mozarteum, though that's not obvious from hearing them. You can't see them. They are hidden on one of the galleries.

At the offertory, he takes pity on an American who has come to stand beside him. The man has pulled out a five-euro bill ready to put into the basket when Siegfried grasps his forearm, shakes his head, and jingles the coins in his own hand. Then he cups his hand around his ear and tilts his head towards the front of the church. The man listens and nods, hearing the rhythmic chink of coins, only coins, as they are dropped into the circulating baskets. He produces some of his own, ready to add to the tune when the basket comes to him. Helping this stranger to fit in is the kind of act of Christian charity of which Siegfried is proud, though he would never boast about it to anyone.

The sermon is delivered by the old priest, which means that Siegfried will be more than usually free to let his mind wander. With some of the younger ones, you would need a notebook to follow what they are telling you, but with the old priest you can listen to the beginning and the end and get the entire message, twice. Today is something about when the sleepers awake. The August sun is pouring through the Romanesque windows that run the length of the church above the rococo riot of frescoes and statuary, and Siegfried wonders how anyone could possibly stay asleep on such a day. He tries to match the story of one of the paintings to his recollections of the bible, but fails. Finally, his eyes come to rest on one of the statues. They are always good for several minutes' contemplation. He loves how their bodies, gilded and stylized, still support heads that are the colours of actual human flesh, mottled rosy and yellow and ruby. Their beards and hair look absolutely real. He supposes they must be horsehair. One day he would like to see them up close enough to determine how they were made. The flesh appears waxy, but he knows it is polychromed wood. For now, he is content to muse about the contrast between the cold abstract body and the warm absolutely individual humanized face, even though both are hard, fixed, unchanging with the years. He looks out over the listening congregation, many of them dressed in traditional costume. From where he stands, he has no view of their faces.

As the service ends, he takes a few steps backward, disengaging slowly from the spell that grips him every Sunday. And that is why he gets hit.

She is the first one out of the musicians' gallery and she is not watching where she is going. He will learn later that she was late for her next playing job. He has never imagined that a violin case, even one of the newer fibreglass ones, could hurt so much, but if it bangs just under the ribs almost anything can hurt. For an instant he thinks she may just pass right on by, but when she is three or four steps past him she suddenly whirls around and meets his eyes. Her face is quite red, a striking contrast to the marble-like folds of her beige dress. *Entschuldigen*, she mutters. *Macht nichts*, he responds, even though it does.

And then she is gone. Eurydice; only she is the one carrying the violin.

Two

He thinks about her as he sips his *verlängerter* in Tomaselli, imagines her, hidden there on the musicians' gallery, her fingers dancing along the neck of her violin to coax those twittering sparrow sounds in the *Sanctus* and the *Benedictus* exactly as Mozart had intended. He only saw her face for a moment. He did not see her hands at all, except in light cotton gloves, one over her mouth just before she said excuse me, and the other clenched around the handle of her violin case. None of this impedes the detail of the vision he conjures.

If he had been quicker he might have invited her for a coffee. She would have seen she owed him that for winding him, and for the bruise he was sure would show up on the flesh above his bottom right rib. Perhaps the *musik direktor* would slip him her name and a phone number, if he stood him to a few rounds at the Stieglbrau.

Sundays, after the *verlängerter*, he crosses the river to walk in the Mirabell Gardens. He makes his way directly to the dwarf garden. He has to cross a little bridge to get to it from the side of the palace, and he imagines it as an enchanted island, even though there is no water around — only a lower park.

There are thirteen dwarves in all. Two of them are women. The disproportion has never occurred to him before today. Only the one with the jug and the bunch of onions and the one whose apron is full of grapes and pomegranates are females. All the others — the fisher with his net, the hunter who is wringing a bird's neck, the drinker with his giant mug, the lazy worker leaning on his shovel — all of them are men. Siegfried stops in front of one of his favourites. This dwarf wears a turban. He is missing one arm and with the other he is pulling hard on a vine against which he has braced his foot. All of the other statues are unambiguously whatever they are, but this one presents a puzzle. He is not hunting, fishing, labouring, shopping, drinking, selling. He is clearly struggling; but against what? For what? What happened to his arm? Siegfried thinks that one of his other favourites, the one that looks like an academic with the spectacles on his nose and his mouth wide open, might be able to help him solve the riddle of the turbaned dwarf — if only he could speak.

They might be Kaiser Karl's dwarves, out on a little holiday from their prison beneath the Untersberg — only he knows they are too grotesque, too comical, to represent those heroic little people. Kaiser Karl's dwarves are only asleep when they are under the mountain. In the air, here, they would be awake and bustling about preparing for the emperor's second coming, not stuck in a single pose, not caught with an unchangeable grimace on their stony faces. They would be, he thinks, like the sleepers awakened in the old priest's sermon this morning.

Lately, vandals have been interfering with the statues. First it was rings of coal smudged like heavy mascara around the eyes of some. Then red paint started appearing on lips. The result is a handful of dwarves who look like they are in drag. Siegfried blamed the gays initially, but now he wonders whether it could be feminists who are defacing, re-facing, the dwarves, trying to achieve a rough gender equity. Whoever is responsible, today he has brought in his pocket some spray cleaner and several rags, and he sets to work rubbing away at the make-up on one of the shopping men. The coal smears, begins to come off, but the painted lipstick will need something stronger. Because of the pits in the stone, the best he is able to do is reduce the look of mascara to the appearance of a five o'clock shadow around the eyes, which might even be natural for dwarves. They always seem quite hairy. Why shouldn't they have to shave around their eyes?

Although he has prepared several speeches to deliver, in the hope that someone might ask what he is doing, they all go to waste. He is the only one in the dwarf garden for the whole forty-five minutes he spends scrubbing. Nobody happens along to be told about how it is a national shame that people deface these products of the Austrian imagination. Nobody gets to listen to his rant against the dilution of folk culture, and how if these statues were more classical, like the groupings representing the four elements in the main garden, vandals would never have dared touch them. Or if they had, someone would have cried foul and cleaned them up right away.

Exhausted, his fingers raw, he deposits the blackened rags in the bin by the stairs. Then he takes solemn leave of each of the dwarves in turn before heading for the bridge back to the main gardens. Rather than walk back past Pluto and Aeneas and all of the others, he turns left up the steps and finds himself in another terraced garden.

He has been here before. The view back over the river and south to the *festung* is a favourite. But today he has come only for the sculpture. It is a bronze. Life-size or perhaps a little larger. A whole different scale from the dwarves at any rate. *Tänzerin*, a small plaque announces. She is a nude, en pointe. One of her hands rests by her side in a gracious curve, while the other is stretched well above her head so that she appears to be pulling herself up by the hair. He thinks of the turbaned dwarf pulling on the vine. And then he thinks once more of the violinist who ran into him in the *Peterskirche*. He knows beyond a shadow of a doubt that without her clothes she would look exactly like this.

Three

Siegfried doesn't very often find himself these days in the part of Bavaria that lies to the north and west of Salzburg across the border. Now and again, he ventures to Berchtesgaden to the south of the city, but since he moved from the depressing apartment in Ainring eighteen months ago he has little reason to go there or to Freilassing or Piding or any of his former haunts. Mainly, he stays in Austria now. He sees this as an important statement to make in the face of the new reality of the European Community with its unpatrolled borders and its creeping homogeneity. He is an *echt* Austrian, the genuine article, born and raised near Krems. He is fiercely loyal. Today, though, the weather is unbearably warm for June, and he recalls that the pool in Freilassing is much nicer than anything in Salzburg. And cheaper.

The swim is refreshing. He goes in twice, lying on the grass in between times. He knows it is foolish to lie and bake when he has come to cool off, but the lawn is dotted with teenaged girls daring one another to bare their breasts to the sun, and he cannot bear to waste that. He remembers one day here with Ingrid, two years ago, how they flirted, swam, flirted some more. She got him to undo the back of her bathing suit top while she lay on her stomach. So there would be no line on her back, she said, but he knew it was really so she could give him little peeks at her nipples as she adjusted her position on the towel beside him. When she took her weight on her elbows, her breasts became twin peaks reflected upside down in a mountain pool. She knew how he loved that.

He does not bother to rinse the chlorine off. They use very little — at least, he can hardly smell it — and he hates the idea of taking a lukewarm shower after the cool freshness of the pool. For no reason that he can later divine, he decides to turn right instead of left out of the *parkplatz*, heading towards Munich rather than back to Salzburg. Perhaps it is the memory of Ingrid's nipples, or mere force of habit that lures him; but at the time he sees it as an innocent whim.

The place is not far along the road, only a little past the turn down for Sillersdorf. He has not even driven past it in eighteen months, not since the day he and Ingrid stood right there and said their official goodbye. It was his idea to make a ceremony of it. He hoped by the dramatic weight of the moment of breakup to validate the whole relationship. It was December. A meeting in the mountains was made too uncertain by the weather. So he had spent nearly a week of lunch hours charting the way the sun came through the mountain, projecting exactly where it would fall at noon on the day he had agreed to move out. They took a picnic, which they had to eat in his car, but precisely at two minutes to noon he guided her to the spot and they held hands until the sun hit them, and then they dropped them. She got into her car, he got into his, and that was that.

As he slows down, about to pull over where he had parked that day, he notices there is someone standing on the spot. He can't be certain it's the exact spot, because it is neither noon nor December. In fact, the entire road-side is lit up, the entire countryside, as if it is a different place altogether. But if it is not precisely the same spot it is not more than a few metres from it.

The person looks up, shielding her eyes from the sun. It is the violinist from the *Peterskirche*. He lets out the clutch and drives past. He will need time to think about what this means.

Four

His friend Hans has a job that Siegfried does not envy. While what he himself does might technically be tour-guiding too, it has none of the demeaning characteristics of Hans's daily routine. Hans tries to soft-pedal the humiliation, insisting he is playing a role just like any actor. He argues that the piece he plays in is educational, uplifting, for those who pay to see it. Siegfried has never paid to see it, so he cannot categorically refute this, though he has his doubts. He cannot imagine how trudging around behind somebody who is dressed like an ancient Celt, listening to them spout propaganda about the salt industry, could be life-improving.

When pressed, he has to admit that Hans is lucky to have the job. Lucky in the sense that a series of apparently random circumstances had to come together to make it possible. The first and most significant of these was the chance discovery, in 1573, of the body of a prehistoric miner, hair, beard, flesh, and clothing all perfectly preserved by the salt he was mining in the Duerrnberg when he died sometime around 400 BCE. Over the centuries that followed, several other Celts, dried like codfish, were found buried in their mine shafts in the Duerrnberg. The discovery nearby of the remains of a Celtic village dating back to 1300 BCE, along with a generally growing taste for history and all things *echt*, and a decline in the fortunes of the salt industry, resulted in a tourist strategy that pays Hans regularly every week from April to October.

Because Hans's job does not pay him well enough that he can look after his car properly, his friends are often called and begged for drives. Today, Hans has promised Siegfried a Zipfer in Hallein if he will pick him up from work and drive him home to Salzburg. Siegfried never remembers that Hans takes at least fifteen minutes to wash off the gunk that is supposed to make him look like he has been preserved in salt for two thousand years, so he has arrived too early and has some time to kill.

He wanders from the mine entrance up to the *Keltendorf*, admiring in solitude the totem pole and the communal oven. Inside the tool house, he tries to wish *Grüss Gott* to one of the wax figures that form the display before recognizing his mistake, and so it is not until he reaches the nobleman's grave that he realizes he is not all alone in the village.

She must mistake him for a tour guide because she asks him what time the village closes.

"I don't know."

"It's just that the mine is already closed, and I drove all the way up here, so I want to spend a little time doing something. You're not about to close up are you?"

"I am not working here."

She blushes. Exactly the shade she turned in the *Peterskirche* when she hit him with her violin case. "Sorry. I just assumed. Have we met before?"

"Not really, no."

"Not really?"

"I think we may have seen one another."

"Oh shit, you're the guy I ran into on my way out of the church the other day. I am so sorry. I had another gig, another job. I'm a musician. But I guess you figured that out, since I bashed you with my instrument. Are you okay, by the way? The case is very hard. I dropped it on my toe once and limped around for a week."

"I am Siegfried."

"Like in Wagner?"

"Like before Wagner even."

"I played *The Ring* last fall. In Toronto. I'm at the Mozarteum now. I'm a Canadian. Most people think I'm American. We like to think there's a difference. I'm Izzy, by the way. Isabel, but everyone calls me Izzy."

"Enchanté," Siegfried says as she holds out her hand. He is pretty sure that he has heard that they speak French in Canada.

"So you're obviously German or Austrian or something. The real thing. What brings you to this tourist trap?"

"I am waiting for my friend. To give him a drive."

"It's not this guy, is it?" she asks, pointing to the skull and bones of the nobleman that lie in the sand along with a few brass rings and other markers of his wealth. "He could be a while."

"My friend is the guide in the mine." Siegfried realizes too late she has made a joke and he should have laughed.

"Not the famous 'man in the salt'?"

"The same."

"I read about this tour, that's why I drove up. I couldn't

believe it. I mean, how hokey can it get? Dressing a guy up like some old Celt so he can take you around a salt mine and spook you out. Don't you think it's pretty hokey?"

"I do not understand 'hokey.'"

"Kitsch. Tacky. Really pushing it, you know, milking the whole thing."

Siegfried would never have imagined he would feel driven to defend Hans's role as the man in the salt, but her tone triggers something. "I think it is important to make some reverence for our history. My friend works very hard. Perhaps in Canada where you do not have this long history it is hard for you to understand."

"Sorry. I didn't mean to make fun of your friend. And there were actually people in North America at the same time your Celts were rooting around in these mountains, by the way. Just so you know."

Siegfried has never been able to cope with this kind of person: the kind who makes him feel he has offended them when they were the ones who started it. He decides to point out some of the landmarks. They look at the twin peaks of Hallein in the middle distance. He hopes she doesn't think he is pointing them out because of their probable resemblance to her breasts as he imagines them beneath her T-shirt. He gestures towards the town of Hallein itself and tells her disgustedly that there are more Turks living there now than Austrians. This statement seems more offensive to her than any awkwardness about the peaks. North Americans cannot understand how complicated Europe is.

As if in answer to a prayer, Hans appears. His skin is pink and radiant where he has scrubbed away the codfish look. "*Grüss Gott*," he says when he sees Isabel, as if unsurprised that Siegfried has hooked up with a beautiful *ausländer* while waiting around the *Keltendorf*.

Siegfried makes the introductions. He can't help feeling a little proud in front of Hans. Like he is responsible for Isabel's existence.

"So you're the famous man in the salt! I missed the tour, I'm afraid. I borrowed a friend's car and I'm not very good with a stick so it took me a lot longer to get here than I expected."

"It is rather silly, the tour." Siegfried has never heard Hans admit this. He feels betrayed.

"I'm sure it's very interesting. It's nice to be proud of your heritage isn't it? Do you know what time the village closes?"

"It is never really closed until dark. Have you had a look around yet? I could give a tour. It is not my job, but I know most of the stories."

"I don't want to hold you up."

"It is no trouble. That is, if Siegfried does not mind. He is to give me a lift."

"I could drive you, if he's in a hurry. Where are you going?"

"I promised my friend here *ein bier* if he came out to get me."

They tour the Celtic village together while Siegfried

wishes he had been quicker that very first day in the church.

"Do you really think the body they found was two thousand years old?" Isabel asks Hans after they have exhausted the sights. "Do you think a body could be preserved that well for that long?"

"The *salz* draws out the wet. It is the wet that corrupts."

"So he was like koshered."

"*Entschuldigen?*"

"Drained, dried out."

"When they laid him out in the church for the people to see, he quickly rotted. They had to bury him nearly right away."

"He was only okay if he stayed underground?"

"*Genau.*"

"I saw the *beinhaus* in Hallstatt. I was playing with the *kurorchester* in Bad Ischl. Now that's a creepy attraction. The *beinhaus*. They dig people up to make room for more, then they clean the bones and paint them and keep them in this little house. Talk about a morbid preoccupation!"

"And in Canada you do not care for your dead?" It slips out before Siegfried knows he is saying it, but he is glad. This girl may be very pretty, but she has some terrible ideas.

"The older people here cannot let go of the past," says Hans. "Our generation, we are more modern." Siegfried is too disgusted to comment on this.

When they get to the *parkplatz*, it turns out she has

forgotten to turn off the lights of her friend's car. Siegfried sits behind the wheel of his Seat while Hans connects the cables and gives her battery a boost. When Hans joins him and announces that he has invited Isabel to follow them to the *biergarten*, Siegfried says nothing. He says little more as they drink their Zipfers, and he offers no argument when Hans says he will stay on a little longer and get a ride home with their new *Kanadian* friend.

Five

The *bergbahnhof* at Sankt Leonhard has a small cafeteria that sells coffee and sandwiches, and a daily special involving noodles and schnitzel. Siegfried usually brings his own food to work. He eats it in the locker room where the operators keep their things. Mingling with the passengers is something he likes to reserve for the ride up the mountain. He is also very careful about what he puts into his body. The signs say that everything they serve is *biologische*, but there is no real evidence. The other workers tend to frequent the cafeteria, hoping to meet an easy American girl or an elderly couple interested in changing their wills. Today, but without any such hopes, he is forced to join them since he left his lunch on the kitchen counter at home.

That is how he knows that Isabel will be on his gondola. From his table, he sees her come into the station and stand in the queue to buy a ticket. She is the only person who is not with someone else, so the line moves quickly and she is soon at the window. There must be problems with communication because it takes nearly a minute before she turns away, ticket in hand, and looks towards the café. He cannot remember telling her that this is where he worked; he doubts that Hans would have. She seems unsurprised, though, to see him sitting at the little round table, and she comes straight over.

"I was afraid I would be late," she says. Anyone casually overhearing might imagine they had a date. Siegfried half expects her then to kiss him on the cheek in the way that girlfriends do. Instead, she sits and helps herself to a sip of his coffee. "Are you driving today?"

"I am always operating the car." It took several months for him to rise to this position and he wants to be sure she appreciates the importance of it. He would not like her to think he ever takes tickets anymore, or manages the gate.

"You left rather quickly last night. Hans said you have to be up early."

Siegfried bets that Hans did. "I must go and prepare the car. *Auf wiedersehn.*" When he looks back, she is shovelling the rest of his lunch into her gorgeous mouth.

ALTHOUGH HE HAS GIVEN the spiel hundreds of times, he finds he is a little nervous today, knowing she is hearing it. The older operators don't bother saying a word unless asked, and then they can only manage in German, but Siegfried likes to provide a prepared commentary, in German and English; it seems more professional. And it gives him something to do. Operating the gondola is not very complicated, though it is important not to admit that.

"Kaiser Karl, who you might know as Charlemagne, sleeps beneath the Untersberg in his underground throne room with his knights and his dwarves around him. When his beard has grown around the great marble table three times, and when the ravens have stopped their circling above the mountain, he will awaken once more to join the final battle between good and evil at the pear tree of Wals. When he has won that battle, he will hang his shield on the tree, and the Golden Age will be upon us." He pauses. "Some believe that Karl sends a nobleman to the surface from time to time to see if the ravens have gone. Perhaps we will be lucky enough to see one of these nobles today." The passengers make the little murmurings that tell him the performance has been a success. He times this for the moment just before the car clears the tower at the two-thirds mark. The little dip and the momentary frissance of panic it creates make a nice period to the Kaiser Karl story.

He decides to forego his usual patter about the orientation of the Celtic settlements around the Untersberg and all that says about the mountain's sacred significance. It always seems an anticlimax, and he does not want anticlimax today.

Isabel brushes by him as she leaves the gondola at the Geier-Ecke. Everyone else manages to navigate the exit without making contact, so he takes this as a good sign. Although he never takes his break outdoors, he decides to follow her onto the mountainside. He has ten minutes before making the trip back down to Sankt Leonhard.

"Can you come for a trek?"

"I must guide the car."

"Of course."

"In fact, I have never been farther than this."

"What?"

"I have not walked on the mountain."

"Never? How can you resist?"

"It is my job to bring people up and take them down."

"But how will you see Kaiser Karl's nobleman when he comes out to check on the ravens?"

"I can see the ravens."

"So I don't suppose you have any advice for me about which trail to follow. Should I go to the ice cave or just as far as the *mittagsscharte*?"

He looks at her feet in their canvas running shoes. "You must be very careful. The walking is not easy."

"I thought you said you had never been."

"People twist their ankles, slip on the loose rock. One time there was a violinist from the *Festspielhaus* who ..."

"Yes?"

"Some of the paths are very steep, I hear. You should try to stay near other people. That is safest."

"How sweet." She kisses him on the forehead and sets

out in the direction of the peak called the Salzburger Hochthron. He stays for a moment at the railing, scanning the landscape below stretched out from the Chiemsee to the Salzkammergut.

Six

Siegfried looks forward to the weekends when he visits his parents in Krems. It's not returning to the womb, but there is a comfort to be found there that he does not find elsewhere. Things continue to go along as they did when he was a child. He knows he can find his father in the *keller*, where some days he tastes wine with a succession of would-be buyers from late morning until dusk. His mother will have starched the curtains in his old room and cooked *tafelspitz* with the apple-and-horse-radish sauce he likes.

This weekend, though, he fails to feel the usual lifting of care as he pulls into the driveway. He cannot stop thinking about Isabel and how, saying goodbye to him after she took the last gondola down, she said she hoped they could walk on the mountain together sometime. To atone for all his previous hesitations, he said yes too quickly. Now they have a date for his next weekday off, which is Thursday. He is not sure what his co-workers will think of his riding the car for mere pleasure. He is not sure how he will cope not being the operator, not being in control.

His mother thinks he looks pale, she worries he is working too hard. He goes to find his father in the *keller*.

A customer, a German from Berchtesgadenland by his licence plate, is just driving away. Siegfried's father stands on the roadside in front of the arched concrete face of the *keller*. It is one of four lined up in a row, burrowed into the hill, each belonging to a different wine family now, though at one time they must all have been part of a single operation. His father's eyes are watery and his nose very red. It has been a long day. They hug. His father takes his elbow and steers him inside the *keller*. It is cold and Siegfried pulls his collar up while his father pours him a glass of *freiheit*. They sit at the little table intended for customers' tastings and his father pours himself some, spilling nearly as much as he gets in the glass.

They do not speak. They do not need to speak. It is good just to sit in this cave under the hillside, drinking his father's wine. Siegfried remembers once bringing a girl here. Their plan was to continue some explorations begun in the field behind the *schule* with French-kissing and some awkward fumbling with buttons and hooks. It was a time when he was sure his father would be out with the vines, and it was the nearest place he could think of. He still marvels at how quickly the girl's skin changed from white goosebumps to blue, and how hard the floor was, even with both coats spread out beneath them. His father had walked in before they were finished — whatever that meant; neither of them had any previous experience. He said nothing, just continued on past them and into the depths of the *keller* where he busied himself with some valves and pipes until the girl (Lillian, her name was) had had time to dress and flee. Then Siegfried had been given a glass of wine — a *burgunder*, rare for his father, nearly the colour of the trickle of blood he knew streaked the lining of his coat where it still lay on the cellar floor.

Siegfried's father falls asleep as soon as dinner is over. After he helps his mother with the dishes, Siegfried heads off to meet up with his friend Dieter as he does weekends when he comes home. Dieter still lives where he always has, though his parents are dead so he has the place to himself. They never stay to drink at Dieter's, but Siegfried joins him there before they go out into the town.

Tonight, he finds Dieter in the kitchen in front of the sink. He has a bright yellow box of Bad Reichenhaller *Salz* that he is sprinkling over his forearms and hands. Siegfried supposes some people might wonder about this. To him, it is normal. He can remember as a boy watching Dieter's father do exactly the same thing. Dieter's is a family of *leichenbestatter*, and, like all careful morticians, they always rub their hands and arms with salt after dressing a corpse. It keeps the hands from falling asleep in sympathy with the dead.

Dieter and Siegfried always go to the same place, drink the same beer, and tell one another the same stories of their youth. The women they meet are not the same from one time to the next, though they might all be sisters for all the apparent difference. They are invariably blond, though seldom naturally so. Their makeup is perfect, though it might be heavy if you saw it in broad daylight. And they wear those filmy print blouses that give you a soft-focus view of their black bras. Siegfried's mother would not approve. She would say they are fast women, aggressive women. But they seldom express an opinion. Some hardly speak. They are medical receptionists or dental hygienists or office clerks, and all they want is what Dieter and Siegfried usually want: companionship, a little exercise, reassurance that they are attractive to another human being.

It is understood that at about eleven o'clock they will invite the evening's pair of women back to Dieter's for a schnapps, and when they get there Dieter and his partner will vanish upstairs, leaving Siegfried and his to improvise on the couch. Sometimes the woman who goes with Dieter will spend the night and Siegfried will have to drive his woman home in Dieter's car before he returns on foot to his parents' house. Sometimes he will drive both women home. There are never any hard feelings or bad scenes. It is an arrangement that suits everyone. If they do meet up again and end up in bed some other weekend when Siegfried is home, nobody ever mentions the last time.

Tonight, Siegfried cannot stop thinking about Isabel, and so at ten-thirty he announces that he has a headache and has to go home. This could be a problem because they have driven in Dieter's car, but the woman who has been flirting quietly with Siegfried offers to take him. They leave Dieter looking completely disoriented by this variation from routine.

Siegfried is about to give the woman directions, but she says she knows. They say nothing more during the ten-minute drive. He feels he should try to kiss her when she stops the motor after she has pulled up on the shoulder in front of the *keller* (he has advised her not to try the driveway). After all, he has spoiled her chances for the night. But she stops him from connecting with her lips, giving him instead her cheek. As he lifts the handle to open the car door, she tells him good night. "It's Lillian, by the way," she adds, and then she starts the engine and it is all he can do to get out before she pulls away.

Seven

"Are those the ravens? You know, the ones you talk about in your spiel?" They have started along the path from the Geier-Ecke *bergbahnhof* in the direction of the Salzburger Hochtron. Siegfried is too busy concentrating on placing his feet to look up. "Or is it the golden eagles? I read about them the last trip. There's a family of four. Did you know? They've been clocked at three hundred kilometres per hour in descent. For the kill. Could eagles like that have scared the ravens away? And what would that mean for Kaiser Karl?"

He is pleased she remembers his tour-guiding from her first trip up the mountain. Today's operator spent the whole trip murmuring to a friend in *Bayerische* so thick Siegfried only understood every third word. This left the passengers to find their own focus, which turned out to be mainly on what they were going to do tomorrow. "They could be the griffon vultures," he tells Isabel. "From the Hellbrunn Zoo. They fly up here."

"From way down there?" She turns back towards the Geierecke peak to look down on Salzburg. "God, the fortress looks so small, doesn't it? When you're climbing up to it, that mountain it's on seems the biggest thing in the world. Do you think they were people once?"

"Who?"

"The birds. You know, like in Ovid. *The Metamorphoses*. People are always turning into birds."

"When they don't turn into trees." Siegfried is glad his mother made him read so much as a child.

"Exactly. I'd much rather become a bird than a tree, wouldn't you? Think what it would be like to have bark start creeping across you, sealing up all your … you know, openings."

After this remark, they are both quiet for a hundred metres or so. They do not know one another very well. For his part, he is trying to remember whether anyone who gets turned into a bird in Ovid is actually being rewarded, or are they all being punished somehow? This helps him take his mind off imagining Isabel's openings.

"I did a Classics degree. Before the music. It's not every man who knows his Ovid. I'm impressed."

"I studied music too. We all study music." He doesn't know why this has come out in such a defensive tone.

"Of course. You came to the Sparrow Mass."

"I go to the *Peterskirsche* every Sunday."

"You don't care either way about Mozart?"

"Everyone loves Mozart."

"Did you study a particular instrument?"

"The accordion."

"Oh."

He has heard that "oh" before. In his *musik schule* there was a bitter rivalry between the *klassisch* and the *volks musik*. The *volks* always won out for funding and support, but the classicists held on to the high road and delivered monosyllabic judgments that made you feel five centimetres tall. "I think it is important to keep for the future our *kultur*."

They have to concentrate as they ascend the next slope. He uses the cable that is anchored in the cliff face to steady himself. She takes his arm, which makes him think his playing accordion may be forgiven, especially since he also knows his Latin literature.

"We can have our picnic at the *mittagscharte*. I saw a perfect place the last time. Only I didn't have anyone to share it with." She rubs her cheek against his shoulder before letting go of his arm as they reach the crest of the slope. "At least, I think it was the *mittagscharte*. It seemed like it must be. You can't really tell when you're there, can you? Maybe if you're there right on December twenty-first. But it's all about how the light hits somewhere else, right? Through this notch."

"The Untersberg has very many associations with light." He does not want to remind her that he has never been to the *mittagsscharte*. And he does not want to think about that place on the side of the road where the sun hits in a narrow beam at the winter solstice. And that is why he ends up starting to tell her the story of Isais.

"I never heard of Isais."

"She was the daughter of Isis and Set."

"The same Set who murdered Osiris and cut him into a dozen pieces?"

"I don't know."

"Well, Isis was Osiris's wife, so it's probably the same guy. But I don't remember her getting together with Set. I thought she hated him for what he did to Osiris. Besides, he was supposed to be infertile, a desert god, wasn't he?"

"I only know what I have been told." Siegfried wonders whether he should stop the story before it really begins. His grandfather told it to him as though it was some big secret, something to be kept from *auslanders*, but why would that be?

"Okay, so Isais is the daughter of Isis and Set. I'll Google her when I get back to Salzburg."

They bid *Grüss Gott* to a middle-aged man who strides past them, flicking his alpine poles purposefully. "I should have started the story with the Crusader. In 1220."

"You mean an actual Crusader. A Templar?"

"On his way home, he had a vision of Isais."

"Pretty eclectic for a Crusader, isn't it? Ecumenical."

"She told him to withdraw to the Untersberg and await her. By the next year, he had built an uncredible series of underground galleries into the mountain. One of them was a temple to Isais."

"What is it with you guys digging tunnels in these mountains?"

Siegfried knows she is talking about the Obersalzberg, the infamous bunkers, but he chooses to ignore the question. There is no answering anyway. "Isais appeared to this crusader — his name was ... Koch."

"You're making this up."

"No. She appeared to Herr Koch several more times."

"What did she tell him — apart from the obvious advice to change his name?"

"The Templars and Herr Koch were ordered to form a secret brotherhood. *Die Herren vom Schwarzen Stein.*"

"Jesus, that's something to do with the SS, isn't it? Way back? I read something."

"Is it? Anyway, the point was they were supposed to wait until a very special ray hit the Untersberg and that would be the dawning of a new age."

"The Ilu Ray, the divine ray. The Age of Aquarius."

"You know this story already?"

"No, but that must be it, mustn't it? You know the song."

He nods, although he has no idea what she is talking about.

When they reach what she thinks must be the *mittagss-charte*, where the path barely clings to the edge of an enormously steep valley, she asks does he want to push on for the ice cave? It is a few seconds before he realizes she is joking.

They sit on a flat rock with their feet on the path so they have to pull them in every time someone passes. She has packed a lunch consisting of two hard-boiled eggs, some kind of white bread that Siegfried has never seen, even in Kaufland, and six cans of beer. He is afraid to ask whether the eggs are *biologische*. Instead, he tells her he is allergic. And cannot tolerate gluten. The beer, however, will be fine.

"I brought a pomegranate for dessert. Can you eat that?"

Even though he knows they are not in season, he says he will try it. She eats both eggs and three pieces of the glaringly white bread while he drains two of the beers. He is amazed to find that she makes no sound when she chews. Like she is not quite human. When they open the pomegranate, the seeds are bare, with just a little green mould forming on some. There is none of the soft red flesh he was looking forward to. How could the fruit form like that, so perfect on the outside and nothing within?

"You're going to be starving, Siegfried. I'm sorry. Shall we head back?"

"We could go on a little way." It is not that he wants to see any more of the mountainside, but on their whole hike he has not yet been able to spot a good place to pee. After the beer, he needs desperately to go.

"Onward, then! To the *eis höhle*!"

"That is too far."

"I thought you said you'd never been around the mountain."

"I have seen maps."

Three hundred metres along, he honestly confesses his need, and leaves the trail to head for some scrubby bushes on the slope below. He slips on some loose rocks at first but keeps his balance and is soon convinced that he is waist deep in greenery, deep enough to unzip and pee. Much later, he will tell himself that it was the noise of his stream hitting the rocks that covered the noise she must surely have made as she clambered down the slope to join him. The ability to chew silently is common; being able to descend a scrabble slope without loosening one stone isn't.

"Me too," she says. "Only it's not such a neat operation for me."

By now he has stopped peeing, though he knows his bladder is not empty.

"It's okay. I didn't look. Not really. Maybe you could do the same?" He hears her zipper and the swoosh of fabric sliding over her hips. "It's tricky on a hill," she laughs, "getting all the angles right."

When he turns around — what man wouldn't? — her

back is to him and she continues to pee for nearly a minute. Then he watches as she carefully fishes a tissue from the front pocket of her jeans. It is not easy with them accordioned around her ankles. She wipes herself, and in one motion stands and pulls her pants back up. He turns his back just before she catches him. He hopes.

"Did you see this?"

He is about to swear he hasn't peeked.

"There's some kind of entranceway. I think it's a cave."

"We should get back up to the path."

"You are afraid of waking Kaiser Karl?"

Isabel has a *taschenlampe* which she shines in front of them as they push the bushes aside and enter the cave. It appears to cut deep into the hillside. She wonders whether it could have been the mine shaft of some ancient Celt. Or one of the Templars' underground shrines he was telling her about. Then she turns off the light and he feels her pressing up against him. Her mouth tastes of spearmint, which surprises him until he finds the chewing gum.

"Sorry," she says. He hears it fly out past his ear and into space.

She is more tender than he would have expected from a girl who jumps a man in a cave. And she keeps telling him there's lots of time, don't hurry it, which annoys him because he hates to be told how to do it. At the same time, it's flattering that she wants it to last. When his moment arrives, he must actually black out for an instant or two because the little moans she is making stop and then start up again before diminishing to sighs and then silence.

"Do you remember Atalanta and Hippomenes?" She has not turned on her *taschenlampe* again. He hears her jeans sliding up over her hips.

"It's something about a race and some golden apples that he throws to slow her down, isn't it?" He is getting tired of Ovid.

"I mean after that. They make love in a shrine hollowed into the bedrock under a temple. The shrine is full of the wooden images of the ancient gods. Remember? Cybele punishes them for the desecration."

"Could we have the light? I can't find one of my shoes."

"She turns them into lions."

"No, it's okay. I found it. We should probably get going. What time is it?"

As they emerge from the cave's mouth Isabel roars quietly into Siegfried's ear, a happy lioness.

If their day could have stopped there, or a few minutes before, when they lay breathless on the cave floor, everything would have been different. This is what he will think in the weeks to come. Now, he is intent on getting back up the slope to the pathway and then back to the *bergbahn* and down to Sankt Leonhard.

They sit on the rock where they ate their lunch, tired from the climb, and from the cave. Her cheeks and neck are red from the roughness of his beard; she has missed a button on her shirt. "Do you ever think of doing anything else?"

"What do you mean?"

"Do you think of going back to school maybe? Of trying a different ... profession?"

The way she pauses, hesitates over how to classify what he does, erases in an instant all fond memories of the cave. How dare she?

"It's just, I mean it's great, I'm sure, and it's responsible work — all those people in your care each trip — but I just wondered whether you ever thought of anything else."

"My father would like me to go into his wine business."

"That could be interesting. Do you ever think of leaving Austria altogether, though?"

Siegfried feels the net closing. It is not something he has much experience with. Mostly, the women he is with in Krems are content to let the sex be sex. But he knows what Isabel is up to. He thinks about what he has read about it in Karl May's books about *Kanada*. "Never." It is better to be honest, not to dangle hopes that are impossibilities.

"This is enough for you, then?"

He does not answer, unsure whether she means their underground fuck or his job on the *bergbahn*.

"I mean it's all very quaint, charming and everything." So she means the job. "But don't you get tired of the spiel, the whole 'Kaiser Karl will come again' thing?"

He looks up just then and sees one of the golden eagles. Or is it a griffon vulture? She asked earlier about the ravens. He has not seen a raven all day.

"A person can get kind of stuck is all I'm saying. You know, like your ancient Celt in his salt mine. Hardened into something else. Now, your friend Hans takes his job with a huge grain of ... well, you know. He sees it as a way to save some money for what he really wants to do with his life."

Siegfried does not ask what she supposes that is. He suggests they begin making their way back to the Geier-Ecke and the gondola.

Where the fog comes from, or why it finds them just as they are approaching the path that branches off up the Salzburger Hochthron, Siegfried does not know. In one of his prepared speeches for the tourists he warns about the changeability of the weather, and there are advisories posted at the stations and along the early parts of the paths. Having never been out on the mountain himself, though, he has not experienced it. They have to move very slowly, testing, making sure before every step, looking up only to try to see the daubs of colour painted on the rocks, there for guidance. Her hand in his grows icy. She has stopped talking, which is a relief, stopped attacking his beliefs, his birthright. The fog thickens. There are voices up ahead. This must mean they are not lost. The voices are speaking his language, but in accents he does not recognize.

Isabel announces that one of her shoelaces has come undone. She lets go of his hand to stoop to tie it. After half a minute, which should have been time enough for her to retie both laces twice, he says her name. No response.

He squats down then and starts waving his arms around to find her. There is only cool mountain air. He straightens up and takes a few steps back the way they have come, whispering her name. Then, although he knows she could not have squeezed past him, he carries on a dozen paces in the direction of the Geier-Ecke, moving towards the voices. He thinks he now recognizes the way they speak. It is a more courtly German, a deader textbook version of what fills the air these days.

How could she have fallen without his hearing? He remembers then her earlier descent to the bushes near the cave, how silently she moved. The voices keep receding ahead of him. He has to follow. From the few words he is able to understand, he can tell they are having a heated conversation about big plans, the future, the dawning of a new age.

A bird suddenly flutters past his ear, up and up. He hears it rising impossibly above him. A small bird. If he didn't know they could never fly this high, he would have thought it was a sparrow.

At the *bergbahnhof*, all of the seats in the waiting room are full, and another dozen people wait anxiously outside. Two loads at least, he thinks. Everyone is talking, exchanging stories of their harrowing adventures in the sudden fog. He listens in vain for the voices he heard before him on the trail, speaking in Old German of a New Day. Only twice does he cast his eyes back out onto the mountain, in case she should still appear.

When they have made Sankt Leonhard, all trips up

the mountain have been cancelled until further notice. The fog is too dangerous. He offers to take the gondola back up for the rest of the waiting passengers, even though it is still his day off. Johann, who is one of his lazier colleagues, readily agrees.

All the way up the mountain, Siegfried speaks to the empty car. He tells, as he always does, of Kaiser Karl and his nobles and dwarves, and of the ravens that circle above the Untersberg. Heroes do not die, he says; they wait beneath the ground to reappear and form new empires. He practises, too, an addition to his regular spiel. He will tell it for the first time on the way down the mountain today with his car full of relieved hikers. It is the story of the returning crusader who met up with the goddess Isais on his way back from Jerusalem, and how she appeared to him again here on this holy mountain.

Lot's Wife

One

They met in the summer after his mother died. Daniel was making a point every weekend of exploring a new part of the province. It was supposed to take his mind off things. He was heading for the old general store in Bass River where there was a weathervane he had heard about. Daniel had no use for a weathervane, had sold his house a few months before, but it made as good a quest as any. His informant was a patient, one of his obsessive-compulsives, who had gone on and on about how beautiful this weathervane was, how cheap. In the end, Daniel didn't get to the Old General Store. He was stopped in his tracks by a woman at the Stone Farm. She didn't usually work right out front, she had said later. This piece was due to be picked up that afternoon, but, since the truck was late, she was putting on some final touches. She confessed to having trouble finishing with things, letting go. There was always a little something more a person could do. The piece was an obelisk of red sandstone, easily six feet high, as big around as a person. Its edges were rough, its top broken off, jagged, but on two of the four faces there were carefully etched patterns. Rows of spirals and concentric triangles were rooted at the base by a crisscross of diamonds. Not that it was the stone that caught his attention first. What he saw first was the curve of the woman's back as she worked with the drill, the thin crescents of moon-white skin that peeked from her cut-off jeans as she leaned into her task. There was a sign, too, announcing Blueberry Hill Stone Farm and Gift Shop, and a parking lot. Without those, he would never have pulled over, not even for that back and those thighs.

He had been watching her work for several minutes when she put the drill down and slid the safety goggles up on her shining forehead. A lock of wet hair flopped over her eye. She pushed it away with the back of her hand.

"Hello."

"Hi. Feel free just to look around. Have you been here before?"

"First time."

"Well, there are gardens all out the back, with the pieces set up in them. The ones that are for sale have little copper flags beside them. Prices should be written on the flags. If you need any help, Callie's in the shop over there."

"I was ... I was looking for something special." He still doesn't know why he said that. He must have been hoping to keep her there a minute longer. Before she could ask him what, he plunged forward. "A monument ... you know, a marker, a ... tombstone."

"I'm sorry."

"My mother. It was a while ago. I had her ... she was cremated." It was important that this woman not think he was too-recently bereaved. The cremation detail was so she also knew he had not kept his mother in a freezer, or in the root cellar like Norman Bates.

"I'm sorry, I don't do gravestones. I mean I have before, but they're trouble. The lettering. Stone isn't very forgiving when you make a mistake. Besides, I only work in sandstone. Most people like something harder, longer-lasting. Granite, for instance. For gravestones, I mean."

Sundials were also something she had done before but was not keen to repeat. She said it was too hard to find a gnomon that worked precisely in this time zone. That's the thing that casts the shadow, she had had to explain. Birdbaths, he would find at the back. And fountains. Callie could help him. She really couldn't take on a gravestone, she was sorry.

"I'm Daniel," he said then, and held out his hand. Hers was hard, dry, covered in grit from the stone she had been working.

"Hi Daniel. I'm sorry about your mother. Look, would you like the guided tour? I'm about finished with this piece anyway, I guess."

Now, sitting beside her as she sleeps on the plane, he wonders again why she did not say her name right away. He tries to remember how many hours went by that afternoon in her enchanted gardens before he learned it. Then it was only because Callie, from the shop, came looking for her. "Percy," she called. "Percy!" Daniel thought she must be calling the cat until the woman sitting next to him on the stone bench answered: "Here. I'm just with a ..." She hadn't finished it. What would the rest have been? A customer? A client? Too soon to say new boyfriend, though Daniel himself knew already by then.

"Persephone," she had explained later. "I hate it, so people call me Percy. It's no better, I know, but at least everybody can hate it equally."

She stirs beside him, dreaming. His professional curiosity is instantly aroused. She never shares her dreams with him, is wary if he asks. "I don't need a shrink," is what she says. "Just a lover." That word comes off her lips too easily, he thinks. There are whole rooms of her she has not let him know, whole volumes of her story that remain closed to him.

The trip to Bermuda was his idea. Although he didn't say so, he hoped it might help them get closer. In the three months since he first showed up at her studio, the relationship had progressed through the usual stages. It had started with an awkward kiss when he got back into his car that first day, passed through picnics where they forgot to eat and came home covered in grass clippings or dandelion fuzz, and settled at four or five nights a week in one another's beds — in Halifax through the week; Bass River on the weekends. But through all of that, he was conscious of her holding back. If she were a patient, he would have made a notation on her chart: emotional hypothermia. Bermuda in October, still balmy while fall's sharp breath started to blow down Nova Scotia's neck, seemed to offer a chance to become what he understood by the word lovers: intimate, without secrets, unfiltered.

She wakes up, smiles, climbs over him to stagger down the aisle to the bathroom. When she gets back, the captain has switched on the seatbelt sign and they spend the rest of the flight craning to catch a first glimpse of the tiny fish hook of islands.

Two

The room is better than he has dared hope. You can never be sure, with the internet. Anything can be made to look good now. They have their own kitchen, a big bathroom, a bed-sitting room. Only the tops of two royal palms interrupt their view of the water, turquoise within its ring of foam-wreathed reefs, and, beyond those, the deeper blue of the open sea. Daniel knows the island quite well. He spent several weeklong vacations here with Jan over the years. It was an easy destination, the flight from Halifax so short. He has not shared much about his ex-wife with Percy, who has never asked, but he has talked a lot about his previous visits to Bermuda. It was a way of getting them both excited about the trip, he thought.

Staying on the South Shore is a new experience for him. With Jan he always stayed in the modest-but-lovely guesthouses that promised to show their guests the authentic Bermuda. When Percy asked would they be staying right on the beach, he had automatically said no, that Bermuda wasn't Cuba or the Dominican, but they could easily walk to the beach. Then he thought about it and did some searching, and so here they are: on the South Shore, with a beach down the cliff below them, and, to their east, a pool where they could order drinks and put them on their tab. There is also their own private balcony with a view to the south that would make you believe in God.

He is about to say exactly this about the view when Persephone lets out a yelp.

"What's wrong?"

"The mould. Mildew. Whatever. Black stuff. Look, along the base of the wall."

"It goes with the climate, I'm afraid; and the building materials. Everything's made of stone. Limestone, quarried on the island. Condensation is a problem — vapour barriers and so forth."

"The houses are made out of the same thing the island itself is made of." It is a statement rather than a question.

He puts this down to her professional interest in stone. Then she adds: "It's like living in man-made caves, right in the rock."

"I guess it might seem like that when you first think about it." He reminds himself to make allowances for how strange this all must be for her, dealing with this place for the first time.

"I feel like I need a shower. A long shower."

"Um. Actually, water is kind of precious here. They have to catch it on the roofs. The wells are all brackish, salty. I guess there might be Watlington Water in the bathrooms. Then you can shower as much as you like."

"Watlington Water." Again, it does not come out as a question.

"They have a desalination plant, reverse osmosis, something to take the salt out. It makes the well water pretty fresh. Good enough for washing."

"Hurricanes must be a problem, don't you think?"

"Generally?"

"If they catch their drinking water on their roofs. What happens when the salt spray hits the roof?"

He has never thought of this. "I suppose it contaminates the tank." Daniel is relieved when she pads off to the shower. He has not anticipated how hard it might be to explain this place to a newcomer.

She is blotting her hair with a bright orange towel half an hour later when she catches him completely off guard. "I think I'd like to go into town tomorrow. Into Hamilton.

I'd like to look in Trimingham's again. They always had such beautiful woolens."

She has been here before.

Three

They see at once the impossibility. Any sand that may have once made a beach below their place is obviously now deposited somewhere else, leaving only prickly limestone crags and slippery troughs scooped out of the coral. With the surf running, they would not find their footing to walk along to the next stretch of beach. Percy is fascinated by the sitting areas perched at intervals along the stepped path down. Concrete has been poured directly onto the rocks to make plateaus. The coral, though, has already begun to resist, crumbling away beneath its new mantle. There has been a rockfall, too — recent, judging by the bright whiteness of the scar in the cliff's face. The huge piece that sheared away sits now where the path might once have been found. Daniel suggests they go around by the road, making it sound like a new idea though it was what she had suggested all along.

"It's not far; you look for the lane marked 'Astwood Walk,'" the bellman had told them. "It's much safer that way."

Astwood Walk is safe but it is also breathtaking: an old Tribe Road, one of many cut across the island's back by its earliest settlers. Through the crumbled asphalt topping, the scraped white coral of the original road is still visible. The oleanders form a perfect arch as they must have done for nearly four hundred years; the sound of the waves never varies from age to age. Then, suddenly, the water appears, its flecked azure framed in the pink flowers and deep green leaves. At the top of the steps, the dry paddles fallen from the bay grape snap under their feet.

They don't see the men until they have begun their descent. The surprise is equal on both sides. Daniel nods, says "afternoon," dropping the "good" and broadening the vowels a little as he has heard the locals do. Percy speeds up and almost misses a step. Her nails dig into Daniel's forearm and she hangs on tight until they have kicked off their sandals on the beach.

"What are they doing up there on the cliff?" she whispers.

"Drinking. Smoking. Staying cool. Who knows? Watching for people to leave their stuff unattended?"

"Not with a hundred steps between."

"You counted?"

"It's creepy, them up there on the edge like that."

"Let's swim." Despite the barrier of one hundred steps, Daniel is careful to leave their things just above the border between wet and dry sand (he knows the tide is going out), near enough that he could run up to save them from would-be thieves.

Persephone moves through the water as if it is her native element. It makes him nervous and excited by turns. He is never comfortable beyond where he can touch bottom, and the surf makes him nervous, too, though he quickly learns from her to turn side-on to the breaking waves.

There is a pair of kettles not far out — small reefs, scooped out like saucers with smoothed coral rims. Percy dolphins straight for them, using the rise of the swell to launch her onto the top of one. She teeters for a moment and Daniel is afraid. What if she slips and hits her head? He is ashamed that what worries him most is that he might have to swim out there to rescue her.

"What do you think this was?" she calls, her voice barely carrying over the waves. She is standing beside a waist-high box. Although it looks like the rest of the kettle — mineral-brown, worn — it is obviously man-made. A couple of rusty pipes protrude from one side.

"Water intake?" he calls back. They both look back at the cliff. Intake for what?

She spies some parrot fish snacking around the kettle, beckons him to join her, then swims back in when he refuses. They bob and talk. Daniel tries not to be too obvious in his glances at their stuff where it lies on the beach, and he never once looks up to the top of the cliff to see if the men are still there.

Their beach is the first of several they are able to walk along with only minor excursions into the water or scuttles over gnarled fingers of rock. At the end of the string, a half-a-dozen plastic patio chairs form a ragged semicircle on the sand. Behind them is a set of steps choked by bay grape. A green plastic garbage can with six faded, folded beach umbrellas sits on the bottom step. You can only just make out the black letters scrawled on the green plastic: "Please leave umbrellas here when finished." The chairs are no longer white, their once-shiny finish pitted by salt. One has a broken seat; another, a cracked arm. It seems obvious that nobody has sat here for a very long time. Daniel and Percy are the only ones on this piece of beach — the only ones for hundreds of metres along the whole stretch. She shivers, and he puts his arm around her shoulders for the walk back, even though he can feel the sweat trickling where their skin touches.

"I suppose they just closed down one day. Just locked the doors and forgot to bring in their umbrella can," she says a few hours later, after they are back at their room, having first dipped in the pool to rinse the salt off.

"And the chairs," says Daniel, handing her a drink — gin on ice, the condensation glistening already on the squat glass. Apparently, she nicked two tiny bottles on the plane when the cart was left unattended in the alcove by the bathroom. Tomorrow, he has promised, they will buy a bottle of Gosling's Crystal. He did not know until now that she drinks gin.

"Perhaps the chairs just toppled over the cliff. They didn't look much like proper beach chairs."

For some reason, Daniel senses that it is important to agree with her on this, though it is so obviously not what happened.

Four

Trimingham's is no longer there. There is only the hole in the ground where it once stood. In the water in the bottom of the hole, several workmen are laughing at one of their colleagues who has fallen over. He is splashing around, pretending to swim.

"It must be quite a bit below sea level," Daniel says.

Persephone does not respond. She has gone white and silent since they came upon the excavation. Daniel feels sorry that the store is no more. He used to like to run his hand down the piles of Shetland sweaters, finger the silk ties. Once, he bought a pair of Bermuda shorts and the long socks that go with them, but it seemed an affectation off the island and he gave the socks to Jan. All of this he remembers with a faint twinge of loss. Percy's response to the absence of Trimingham's, by contrast, verges on full-blown mourning. How could the store have meant that much to her? How many times, exactly, had she been here?

The morning started full of promise. They waited only a few minutes for the number seven bus, which went right by the gates of their place. When they reached the terminal, there was a number eleven (St. George's via the Caves and Aquarium) waiting two bays down. Daniel had to stand after North Village, but he didn't mind because it meant he could feel Persephone's breath, cool on his forearm as he held on to the back of the seat in front of her. Flatt's was not far.

At the aquarium, the woman in the ticket booth stood up to scan the floor around their feet, looking desperately for children since she had, without asking, already rung them in at the family rate. Daniel thought Persephone might be offended, feel pressured by the woman's mistake, but she only smiled and shook her head. At the same time, she squeezed his hand in a way that might have said "maybe sometime."

The fish tanks held little interest for her. She paused only briefly at the North Rock environment with its impressive groupers and sharks. A sudden downpour ruled out the zoo and they ran for shelter in the small museum at the centre of the complex. Daniel calculated that he and Jan may have spent a total of five minutes on these displays over three or four visits, but Percy was enthralled. She lingered over every caption. Daniel discovered a huge variety of things he did not know he did not know. He learned how much of the island's vegetation had actually arrived only in the past few hundred years, as seeds in bird's bellies; and how a number of marine species had come north as larva in the Gulf Stream, the same Gulf Stream that had delivered lion fish dumped out of fish bowls in Florida. She read to him that skinks — black lizards, the display informed them — were rafters, meaning they had boated here on bits of flotsam. The obvious underlying theme was that the word indigenous had very little meaning here. There weren't even any people until the seventeenth century. All were invaders, all invaded. Now, in the Great Sound, there was a project to return one whole island to a condition of pre-Colonial vegetation. Daniel did not add what he did know about this kind of thirst for purity. For decades in the mid-twentieth century, resorts in Bermuda had been carefully coded for travel agents as "Hibiscus" or "Oleander." One took Jews. The other did not.

The geological display interested Percy most. There were buttons you could push to make a map light up. Pressed in sequence, they told a story that began with an ancient volcano and progressed to a land mass that stretched all the way out to what is now lonely North Rock before it dwindled into a string of three-hundred-and-sixty-five islands, one for every day of the year. "What about leap year, mister?" Daniel had asked the taped commentator. "Just wait. There will be a new one break off any time," Percy had replied.

Now, as they stand before the hole that was Trimingham's, Daniel understands what she meant. It is funny, he thinks, that somebody who makes her living by transforming blocks of stone should resent Mother Nature for doing the same.

"They'll build something tall here. It used to be that the Bank of Bermuda was the tallest building. And that was only because they had to build it taller than Butterfield's Bank. But now there are half a dozen as tall. Imagine. The buildings are getting bigger, while the land mass is actually shrinking."

They end up in the souvenir shop near the bottom of Queen Street. It has an unpronounceable Dutch name.

Daniel cringes as he compares the place to his memories of Trimingham's, but it actually seems to cheer Percy up. She begins to mock the awful gewgaws that line the shelves. The diatribe is hilarious, but Daniel feels sorry for a young couple who are obviously hurt when they overhear. Finally, Percy announces that she will not leave without a towel she is waving in his face. She has found it by sliding back the door on a cabinet underneath the display shelves. Daniel tells her the hotel will provide as many beach towels as they want. "They never dry here," he says. "The salt gets in them and you have to wash them or they'll never dry. The hotel laundry won't wash this thing for you." In the end, he simply nods while Percy continues to point out the towel's charms on their way to the cash register.

"See. That's the *Queen of Bermuda*. It was this old ocean liner, hasn't run for years. Only, look, they've spelled it 'B-U-R-muda,' and look: there's her sister ship the '*Ocen Monarch*,' and a '*Moorgate*.' Not a Moongate, a Moorgate. Like Othello." She fumbles for the label. "Right. Just as I thought. Made in you-know-where."

The girl at the cash looks uncomfortable, wants to know how they found the towel. She thought they had gotten rid of them. It was old stock. Couldn't she interest them in something a little newer? She had one with a Bermuda Fitted Dinghy they could have for the same price.

"I want this one. It has sentimental value."

"They made some mistakes," the girl says.

"So have I."

Five

Daniel hates walks that make him sweat. Sweating, he thinks, is for real exertion — running, or squash, or a hundred sit-ups — not for something everybody does simply to get around. Even this early in the morning, the heat is thick; you could cut it. His shirt is plastered to his back, there's a wet patch the shape of a pear over his sternum.

"It's just a little farther. You'll love it."

He has grown used to the way their roles have reversed. She is now the tour guide and he the tourist. What he learned of the place in his handful of visits with Jan would barely account for the thickness of a page compared to the volumes she seems to know. When he asked her finally last night how many times she had been here, she had taken a long time to answer. Then: "How would you count living here?" For four years, she had admitted when he insisted, but beyond that she would say nothing. They made love, even though he was hurt by this sudden reminder of how little he knew her. There are some things he can't turn down.

When they arrive at the gates, he remembers seeing them before, from a bus or a motorbike. They are crumbling, grey, sponge toffee, but someone is obviously careful to keep the vegetation back. He can still read the letters on the marble insert: "Southlands."

They have been reading in the issues of *The Royal Gazette* that arrive every morning at their door about the controversy over the property. A developer is looking for a special government order to bend the rules so a big company from Dubai can build a hotel. One of the critical problems for the development is that the South Shore Road cuts the majority of the property off from the beach. So they want to divert the road underground to make life more convenient for the hotel guests. Then there is the structure itself: steel and glass, no traditional materials. It's a beckoning target for a hurricane, some say. This last item is what has captured Percy's imagination. When he read to her about the proposed tunnel for the main road, she couldn't muster an ounce of righteous indignation, but the vulnerability to hurricanes got her going immediately. "They have to be stopped," she said. "Can't they learn?"

Ten feet up the driveway, Daniel finds it hard to remember ever being anywhere else. The oleanders and bougainvillea form a thick canopy overhead. At eye level the huge exposed roots of the banyan cloister them in a jungle like nothing he has ever seen. Even the road noises die off.

"I told you it would be worth the walk. This is the last place on the island where many of these plants still live. The last wilderness. It has been like this as long as I can remember."

"But people lived here once? It was an estate. The gates —"

"Nature took it back. You can't stop it growing here, you know: the plant life. The mineral decays, but the vegetable keeps on forever."

They continue up the drive without speaking, the symphony of the tree frogs loud in their ears. It is shaded enough here that they sing all day without stopping, she tells him, sing till they burst their hearts and die.

Where the driveway curves, there is a broken stone wall and, at a much lower level, a terraced space, still kept clear. It must have served for tennis or croquet once. Daniel is about to say something about the oddness of this one mowed section in the wilderness when they spy the motorbikes. They are parked in the unkempt hedge of frangipani. There is a notch carved out with the hard-edged signature swipes of a machete. Behind the bikes, the cutting takes a sharp turn into what must be a walkway or steps.

"Hellow? Morning," sings a voice from a little above them.

Percy freezes.

Niobe, Daniel thinks, turned to stone. "Morning," he calls back. Then he takes Percy's hand, leads her back the way they have come.

Six

They don't talk about it until later that afternoon. On the beach. After a swim.

"I just didn't know who it was, that's all. That voice. All of a sudden from up above us like that. Like a ghost."

"I was afraid you were having some kind of, I don't know, seizure."

"I froze. It was a shock, that's all. A surprise."

"That people still live there. It's not so much of a jungle after all."

"Yeah. That was it."

But Daniel can tell it wasn't.

Percy produces a bottle from her bag.

"If I had known, I would have brought some ice. And a couple of glasses."

"It's from the souvenir shop."

He recognizes it then: a tiny bottle of pink sand she insisted on buying, despite the ridiculous price.

"You're liberating it?"

She has already unscrewed the cap. A trickle of ground coral is caught by the wind and sprinkled over an area a foot square.

"Did you notice that shelf of sand near the bottom of the steps?"

Of course he noticed. They stood on the edge and let gravity give them a ride down the two-foot drop, laughing and doing it twice more.

"That shelf wasn't there yesterday, that face of sand. The beach is constantly changing. I am just taking part in the process."

"Three pinches of sand will make a difference?"

"How do you know they won't?"

"Are you going to refill the bottle at least?"

They walk down the beach, coming once again upon

the semicircle of decaying white chairs. Someone has had a fire overnight. The charred remains of a couple of large pieces of lumber make a sharp contrast with the sand. There is a faint whiff of smoke.

"Where would they find the wood?" Daniel wonders. "Would it have drifted? The pieces look awfully big. And dry."

"Did you see those stairs back there? The ones that just stop halfway down the cliff?"

He has been puzzled by them each time they have passed.

"There used to be a hotel up there. The beach house was built right into the cliff. It was stunning. I suppose there are still parts of it up there. Beams or joists or something."

"What happened?"

"A hurricane. The beach never stays the same. I told you."

As they wander back towards Simmonds' Beach, she points out three more blemishes on the cliff face. She can name each one, tell him the years when the buildings fell to the beach and were mostly cleared away.

He does not ask her why she knows all this. He waits. After they have been lying in the sun in silence for half an hour she begins to tell him. The towel from the souvenir store is over her face. Its little Gombey Dancer trembles a little, but does not actually dance.

"They used to serve dinner. The food wasn't anything special, but it didn't matter. It was our favourite place.

The view over the South Shore, you never tired of look-ing at it. He loved it here."

Daniel does not ask who "he" is.

"We came for little occasions, big occasions. We were living nearby."

On the Southlands property, no doubt in whatever little cottage was tucked behind that frangipani hedge. Daniel understands now her moment of shock.

"The staff knew us, made us feel at home. I think they were always so glad to see people who weren't really tourists. It was the last place we ate."

"I'm sorry. Breakups can be …" He thinks of the months of stinging eyes and burning throat with Jan as they drifted and then blew apart. He wants to tell Percy that she will recover, that people move on.

"We had the place nearly to ourselves. It was amazing they were open at all, I guess. With all the warnings. He loved the dry rustle of the palms. There were palms up there; you wouldn't believe it now. We had to hold on to our napkins the whole time. Part of my salad actually blew away. The wind was heavy with salt and heat. If I had known it was the last, I would have made us stay for dessert."

Percy stops, takes the towel off her face, begins fill-ing the souvenir bottle, by turns pushing it neck-down into the sand and turning it upright to let the grains settle. When the bottle is full, she dumps it out again. With this makeshift hourglass, she tells off several silent minutes before she speaks again.

"Peter worked at the Biological Station. In the east end. It was a long ride, but we loved our little cottage. People said afterwards he should not have been out on a motorbike that day. But he rode to work in all weathers. People said, but never to my face, that he shouldn't have been trying to get in to work at all. It was a hurricane. If he'd worked in a business, it would have been closed. Peter used to say that biology never closed. You know the causeway? We came over it on the way from the airport."

"Oh my God. I remember hearing about that on the news. Even in Halifax." Daniel does not ask if they ever found the body. That was part of the attraction of the story. The news agencies kept the tragedy alive for several days while the search dragged on. "We should probably get out of the sun soon." It is all he can think to say. Stupid.

"You go on up. I just want to stay a little longer. It won't be the same beach tomorrow."

He looks down when he has reached the top of the hundred stairs. She is standing just where he left her, looking out to sea. Stock still.

Spilling the Salt

I told Martin I didn't want a housewarming. "We're a little old, don't you think?" I said. "And there's something pathetic about a party you throw for yourself, guilting all your friends into bringing you presents, stuff we don't want or need."

"Then we'll say it's best wishes only. No presents. A housewarming is about warming the house anyway, filling it with your friends for the first time. It's not about gifts."

"I thought everything was about gifts with you people."

"This particular thing is about friends."

When we began making the invitation list, though, I began to wonder whether we should have made the party about gifts after all. So many old friends had to be scratched off. They were either my friends from before, or his. There were so many combinations that would not work. Like any new relationship, ours had left behind a wake of old ones. The party was shaping up to be one grim evening-long reminder of that. So we were delighted when Rupert asked if he could bring along a guest. No, we didn't know her, he said. It was hard to imagine who she might be — Rupert kept pretty much to himself — but one extra body would plump things up, and the guest list was looking anorexic.

Peter was the first to arrive. He had been camping, and he came through the door armed with a bath towel, his shaving kit, and a cotton grocery bag bulging with clean clothes. "I'm early, I know. I wondered if I could maybe, you know, grab a shower?"

"At least he didn't bring a gift," I whispered to Martin after he had shown Peter the bathroom and explained the peculiarities of the taps. I knew all Martin could think about was the glistening porcelain he had worked on so hard that afternoon, how it would soon be sprinkled with shed pubic hairs, and how he would have to slip away to swab the tub before the first guest needed to pee.

Claire came straight in without bothering to ring the bell. She said she thought we would be too busy with our other guests to answer the door. I looked around at the empty living room and laughed.

"Have you left the water running somewhere?"

"Peter's having a shower."

"If I'd known it was that kind of party I'd have brought my laundry along. What would Frazer have to say about Peter's getting naked in your new bathroom, I wonder, lathering his golden boughs? There must be some culture somewhere where that's actually traditional for warming a house, right Martin?"

I watched Martin cringe as he thought again of Peter's pubes circling our freshly Chloroxed drain.

Claire produced a bottle of wine from her enormous purse, apologizing that it wasn't wrapped.

"You weren't supposed to bring anything."

"I couldn't show up at an anthropologist's house-warming without a gift. Besides, I want you to try this. I think you'll be amused by its legs or something." Claire was wearing a short skirt, and she struck a pose for empha-sis. Martin almost missed it reaching for the glasses.

When Peter emerged in a cloud of steam, we found him a glass. Claire poured. I have trouble sometimes. "Nice bouquet," she said, sniffing at Peter's wet hair. "Did you help yourself to Liz's shampoo too?"

"I brought my own. In fact, I think I left the bottle in there. There's only a bit left in the bottom."

"That can be your housewarming present."

"Shit. The invitation said no presents."

"It's okay, Peter," I said. "Claire's joking."

By the time Rupert and his guest arrived, the four of us had already polished off the bottle of Shiraz. Martin quickly opened a Merlot and found two more glasses. The introductions at the door had been disastrously awk-ward and he was obviously hoping to smooth things out as soon as possible.

The awkwardness had started with Rupert's introduc-ing Sophia all around without mentioning her last name or hinting at what their relationship might be. It was as though he wasn't in possession of any more specific information than we were on either score, almost as though he had picked her up on the way in — only he had told us she would be coming. Sophia, who is apparently one of those people who are always trying desperately to make connections, said she thought she recognized Martin. She worked with Sherry, she told us, and Martin and Sherry were connected somehow, weren't they? Something about a friend of Sherry's. The name would come to her in a moment. To head off the inevitable epiphany, Claire offered to show her around the house, even though it wasn't hers to show. When they returned a few minutes later, Sophia looked red in the face, and she did not open her mouth for several minutes. Anneke's name remained unspoken in our new house, which I suppose was a good thing, although it wouldn't really have bothered me, I think. I am not the superstitious type.

"IT'S NOT AS SCARY as it looks," Sherry was saying as she poured the last of the pickling salt into the water. "You could pay big money for this treatment in a spa, Anneke. It might look a little different, of course, but the physics is the same, or the chemistry."

"Isn't there something about water and electricity, you know, keeping them apart?" I would freely admit to being a little depressed, but I was a long way from engineering my own death. I wished the battery charger had stayed in the garage, far away from the dishpan full of salty water. I wished Martin had taken it when we divided everything up.

"It's all under control."

"An old piece of copper pipe and a nail doesn't look so professional. We could go to a spa. I'll pay."

But Sherry had dropped the electrodes into the water and was pulling up a stool. "This is going to be great for you. Draw all the toxins out."

"I'm divorced, not poisoned."

"The stress. The toxins build up. You'll see. This draws them out through the pores in your feet."

"Why does it have to be my feet?" I hate my feet. I won't wear sandals even on the hottest days. It's the toes, mostly: peasant's toes, wide as they are long. My big toenail is a square window with little curtains of fat on either side. Sherry has perfect feet: toes long as fingers almost, the second one extending longest of all. That is sexy.

"Come on, Anneke, you need this."

I rolled my socks down, easing them slowly over my heel, taking a deep breath, and then whipping them off. God. Those awful toes.

"Sit. Now put both feet in at once."

"This is really safe?"

"As houses. Churches. Whatever. And you're going to feel so great: more energy, more vitality. You'll be more aware."

"I don't want to be more aware. Couldn't we have a nice bottle of wine instead? What I really want to do is forget."

"It's time to get on with your life. Martin is getting on with his."

"Fucking Martin. They're having a housewarming tonight, did you know?" And so I sat on the stool and plunged both of my peasant's feet into the tub. Maybe electrocution wasn't such a bad plan after all.

"YOU REALLY WERE NOT supposed to bring anything. We said on the invitation."

"This is practically nothing. Ask Rupert."

It was the first time I had ever seen a depression-glass hen saltcellar, though I certainly didn't know at the time that's what it was. Its appearance gave no clue about its function, which I think might also be a decent definition of ugly.

"I bid quite a lot, on the internet. It's a kind of obsession. They're collectible. I was pretty sure you wouldn't have one." Sophia was obviously one of those people who always have to apologize for doing something nice.

"They really are a popular item," Rupert said, eager to support his date, even if he had not bothered to introduce or brief her properly. "I can barely keep them in the store." He twitched when he said it, so I knew it was a lie. He would never offer such a ghastly thing for sale in his beautiful shop. "This is a very fine specimen. Depression glass, you know."

"It's for salt, right?" Martin asked. How does he guess these things?

"Of course for salt," I snapped, trying to make it

sound as though Martin was way behind. "We only have shakers. This is terrific. Exactly what we needed. But you shouldn't have."

Martin had told me about his wedding day with Anneke, the fleur de sel they had bought to sprinkle in their pockets, their shoes. This hideous hen would be a perfect vessel for that stuff. He and I had agreed to skip all those stupid superstitions. Our marriage will last, or it won't. A few grains of salt aren't going to tip the balance.

Already I was trying to think of where I would hide the thing, and wondering whether Martin would make me keep it on display. Or fill it with lucky salt.

"If the hen is for salt, what's for pepper?" asked Claire.

"THE WATER LOOKS EXACTLY the same to me."

"Give it time. Those toxins are really built up in there, I guess."

"Maybe my feet don't work right. The pores."

"This works on everybody."

"You've done it before?"

"I've read about it."

I knew better than to challenge this. Sherry would always trust her reading over any amount of experience. "The colour tells you something?"

"Orange is for toxins from the joints; brown and black for the liver."

"It sounds like Galen or somebody. Wasn't he the one with the humours — black bile and yellow bile and choler and all of that? Why did our teachers think we needed to know all that stuff to understand Shakespeare?"

"Look, is that a black fleck?"

"My feet weren't all that clean, actually."

"Or it's heavy metal. I think it's heavy metal. Heavy metal is a great sign."

"Wow. I haven't listened to that stuff in years. I see. This really is going deep into my being and flushing things right out."

"If you're not going to take it seriously ..."

I have to admit I was touched by Sherry's concern, even if the ionic footbath was a lot of crap. "Sorry," I said. "I am taking it seriously. Really."

"I'll get us a beer."

"Is it safe for me to drink while my feet are in a tub of water with two battery leads? Forget it. I'd love a beer."

Sherry returned with two Zipfers. She spends crazy amounts for beer; I don't even know how she gets some of the stuff she gets. And her laptop. She prefers conversations where she can simultaneously be somewhere else.

"THERE'S MORE?" I WAS getting sick of the party. Couldn't people read? Couldn't people look around and see that Martin and I absolutely did not need any more things?

"It goes with Sophia's present," said Rupert, defensively. He is always quick to detect tone. I felt bad, but only a little.

"Aha! The little salt hen's pepper cock," said Claire.

"What? No. It's ... well ... unwrap it, Liz."

"You do it, Martin."

As soon as I suggested this I regretted it. Martin is the slowest unwrapper I know. And I wanted the whole thing to be over so we could be alone, maybe make love somewhere unusual. That would be the real housewarming. The party had been supposed to be foreplay, I suddenly realized; and it was rotten.

"You've probably heard all about this guy."

"Rupert, you're going to give it away," said Sophia.

"That's okay, Rupert." I hoped maybe Martin would not need to finish the unwrapping.

"Really? Do you want some help with the paper, Martin?"

"I'm trying to save it."

"Heard all about what guy?" I said.

"Chef Antoine. He's local. Well, not originally of course. He's something European, I think, something like that. Maybe it's Quebec. French. Something like that."

"Something like that," said Claire. "We dated for a while."

"Anyway, he has that new restaurant, the new place downtown. And he's just released this collection of salts."

"Salt is traditional for a housewarming in several Mediterranean cultures. Salt, bread, and wine." I wondered whether Martin was congratulating our guests on their appropriate choices or warning me to bite my tongue.

"MAYBE IF WE LOOK up some stuff on salts, and I read to you. Kind of put your body in the mood, you know. Inspire you." Sherry's fingers were busy already on the keyboard.

"Sure." I thought it might actually help take my mind off the housewarming that asshole and his new (old) wife were having. But Sherry had shifted to another track already, distracted.

"Did I tell you about the Internet café in Salzburg?"

She had, of course, but there was little point in saying so.

"I saw this guy have a major meltdown there, one time, surfing."

"Porn?"

"He was an Austrian, I think."

"Genealogy?"

"Salt. Seriously. Salt. Who gets all bent out of shape about salt?"

"He told you it was salt?"

"His friend was supposed to be on the splash page for this tourist-trap salt mine on the Duerrnberg. I think the guy, the Austrian, was a little jealous. I think he wanted to be able to tell his friend that he wasn't really so famous, so he was doing a general search, you know, to prove it, to see how many clicks it took to get to his friend's picture."

"And you know all this because …?"

"I'd kind of picked him up. Or I was about to. Sometimes with those Germanic types you can't tell. Anyway

I was looking over his shoulder and he wasn't minding that. He typed in '*salz.*' That was it. Just *salz.* It seemed a little harsh to me. I mean the friend didn't have a hope in hell of being within twenty clicks at that rate. So he scrolled through Wikipedia and the industrial sites, and it was looking pretty good because his Duerrnberg friend wasn't showing up in the top ten. But then, top of the next page, he clicked on a site that promised Great Salts of the Globe. I guess he was trying to find out where Duerrnberg would rate on that scale."

"And how did it?" I just threw that in. I really didn't care, but I always like to remind Sherry about the conventions of conversation.

"He didn't find out. It turned out to be some kind of cooking site. They were selling gourmet salts. He freaked."

"He didn't like fancy salts?"

"It was because the company was based in Canada. This guy just blew up. What made a Canadian think he should be selling Salts of the World?"

THE BOX WAS HARD to get open. I tried to take it away from Martin, murmuring that we could explore the contents later; we should be paying attention to our guests.

"This is part of the idea of the gift," said Rupert. He held a plate of cucumbers in his left hand and something shiny in his right. Had he brought the fucking cucumbers with him? I was sure we didn't have any in the fridge; and he hadn't been out of my sight anyway. The cucumbers were placed with a flourish on the coffee table. The shiny thing turned out to be a grater. Like a magician with an egg, he palmed a lump of pink crystal, which he announced was Himalayan rock salt, the oldest salt on earth. It was like being at a bizarre carnival. Rupert, magician and barker at once, rubbed the rock across the grater and it snowed on the cucumbers.

"Should we be writing down our impressions?" Peter always takes notes at wine tastings. He and some of the other men like to out-adjective one another. Women don't bother with that bullshit. We don't have to prove who is biggest. It's obvious with us.

It didn't taste pink, of course. It tasted like salt, although Claire tried to tell us she could smell Edmund Hillary's feet in it.

"IS IT LOOKING A little green now? What would green be?"

"Gallbladder. I don't think it's very green. Yellow maybe."

"That's urinary tract, you said. That would be like I was pissed off or something. Imagine."

"And there's a little foam. That's lymph nodes draining."

"That doesn't sound very good."

"Whatever comes out is good. You don't want this shit all bunged up inside you. You want to make a fresh start, remember?"

My feet were tingling. I knew that when I took them out they would look like prunes. Peasant prunes. "So the Austrian didn't hit you or anything? For being a Canadian?"

"He just stormed out of the café. There was still time on his machine."

"Which you used."

"Kind of. I shared. There was this little Hispanic guy in the café who had been waiting for a machine. He had a violin case with him. Viola, I guess it was. He'd been playing Schubert — 'The Trout.' Not his usual gig, apparently. Anyway, I invited him over to share the screen."

"Jesus, Sherry. You really don't miss an opportunity, do you?"

"You don't know what it's like over there. Anyway, this guy was completely fascinated by the Great-Salts-of-the-Globe site. Have you ever realized how sexy it can be, surfing the net with somebody?"

"No."

"We were very close so that we could both see the screen properly. And I was operating the mouse, scrolling and clicking and making little squeaks with each new salt. I wasn't all that excited about the salts, but he seemed to be into the whole thing. He pressed his thigh a little harder against mine. And then he let his hand drop into my lap."

"You didn't smack him?"

"You had to be there. Probably half the people in the café were surfing porn and we were looking at salt, but it was way hotter. I let him leave his hand there, and kind of moved a little bit to help him."

"He could have been Jack the Ripper."

"We got to a picture of a yellow cylinder of salt. Bad Reichenhaller. Nothing very special looking. I said, 'that's near here somewhere, isn't it?' But the guy obviously wasn't listening. He was somewhere else altogether. He had to hold his viola case over his crotch to hide the wet spot when he left the café."

WE WERE ON TO the Maldon salt, with no sign of flagging enthusiasm from anyone but me. Claire said she thought it was a bit of a fraud, including it in the sampler, since, according to Antoine, it was something no decent kitchen had been without for at least a decade. It hardly counted as exotic, therefore.

"But it isn't local. Isn't that the point? It is a 'salt of the globe.' Exoticism is another matter." Peter took a flake and crunched it between his front teeth, waiting for the rebuttals.

"How could you exclude it anyway?" Sophia's cheeks were flushed. She probably didn't drink a lot of wine. "It's so beautiful. The structure." She held a flake up to the light. Everyone else took one too. They all looked at me, so I grabbed a pinch and isolated one crystal and threw the rest over my shoulder. "Each one unique," whispered Sophia, "like snowflakes."

"I don't think that can be right," said Peter. "Surely they must all form the same. That's physics or chemistry or something, isn't it?"

"But they don't look the same. Not exactly." Martin sounded on shaky ground.

"That's from being tumbled about. They wear one another down. An edge comes off here, a point there. But they start out identical. I'm pretty sure."

"They look like little translucent Monopoly Houses. Or tents. Or pyramids. Shelter anyway. Perfect for a housewarming. Thank you, Rupert." Martin looked at me when he finished saying this. I could not tell whether he was putting a nice gracious capper on the salt tasting or rebuking me for not being more grateful.

"I REALLY NEED TO pee, and I don't think that is going to come out through the pores in my feet."

Sherry looked at her homemade ionic footbath. Despondent, I think would be the right word. "It really should work better than this. Yeah, go ahead and have a pee." She handed me a towel to dry my stubby feet. "All I wanted was to help. Martin is such a shit. I don't know how I ever —"

"How you ever what?"

"Didn't see it."

"Banged him, I thought you were going to say."

"God, Anneke. Yuck."

"Careful." I padded to the bathroom.

Poor Sherry. The whole thing had been a bust. I imagine her unplugging the charger and removing the electrodes, shaking her head at the failed experiment. Then she would have hefted the tub and carried it to the

kitchen to dump the salty water, maybe watching hope-
fully for late-breaking signs of cast-off poisons. When I
got out of the bathroom, she was already gone. I wanted
to phone her to tell her I actually did feel better, but I was
afraid she might take it the wrong way.

I HAD NEVER WANTED anything as much as I wanted the
party to be over. I felt ashamed about what I was about to
do, but it was all I could think of. Everybody but Sophia
knew about my condition. For all I knew, even Sophia
had been briefed by Rupert. They would immediately
accept that I was having some kind of a relapse, and
they would slip away quickly and quietly, having first
murmured half-hearted offers of help. Martin would
be in a state for a while, until they were safely out of the
driveway and I could tell him that everything was really
all right; but the party had been his idea, not mine, so
a little suffering on his part did not seem unfair.

"I have to pee," I said, leaving the others to chew over
the economic implications of Chef Antoine's new collection. Peter had reminded them all of how valuable salt
had been up until about a hundred and fifty years before.
Rupert had chimed in about elaborate antique saltcellars
and how they attested to the preciousness of what they
held. Even Martin had done one of his routines about
the anthropological significances of the stuff. Sophia
had not made a contribution, but had nodded vigorously
when Rupert spoke. Then Peter had gone on to describe
how the value plummeted when geological science came

on the scene and pointed out that you could find salt almost anywhere. Except Japan, apparently. Gourmet salts, he said, represented a way of making the stuff precious once more. As I left the room, I made sure to knock up against the doorframe.

"Are you okay?" Martin called out, obviously annoyed to be distracted from the conversation.

"Fine, just fine," I said, making sure it sounded brave, and that they could hear me miss my footing once on the stairs.

When I came back, they were on to a new subject — something about a treatment to draw out toxins from the body using ionization. Peter was arguing that this was yet another way of re-mystifying salt, of putting it back on its pedestal. He had one leg stretched out full-length in front of him, making it hard for me to plot a safe collapse. The glass-topped coffee table could do a lot of damage to my head on my way down, but I wanted to be sure to be able to sweep the salt collection off it as I went.

"The whole thing doesn't sound very scientific," Sophia was saying as I let my legs go to jelly.

"Jesus. Liz! Liz!" Martin had been almost fast enough to get fully beneath me before I hit the rug. I reminded myself of how lucky I was to have him at last. He instructed Claire where to find the syringe and the cortisone. For a moment I wondered whether there might be negative effects from taking the shot when I didn't really need it. Then I decided that whatever they were it would be worth it. Martin was not very practised at sticking me, but I wasn't sure how I could back away now. The doctors had made him practise on an orange, and the orange hadn't died, so I kept my eyes shut and waited.

"What's happened?" It was Sophia's voice. She sounded truly concerned.

"Liz suffers from Addison's disease. She has sudden drops in blood pressure." Rupert made it sound like it was a social disease.

"It's the blood volume. It drops." Claire had obviously been reading up, which would have been touching if I didn't just want her, want all of them, to leave. "Basically, it's in the signalling to the kidneys."

"They waste salt." Martin said it just as he eased the needle in. He put a pillow from the sofa under my head. "She'll be fine in a few minutes, but groggy. I'll help you find your coats."

As I lay on our new living-room floor, rehearsing how I would tell Martin I had faked the attack, I could hear him by the front door, thanking them all for coming, thanking them all for their gifts to warm the new house.

Acknowledgements

"Jesus" first appeared as "Bad Men Who Love Jesus" in *The New Quarterly* 86; and "Proserpina" first appeared in *The Fiddlehead* 224.